WEDDING VIOLET

FAIR CYPRIANS OF LONDON

BEVERLEY OAKLEY

CHAPTER 1

"Gad's teeth, that was the best tupping I've ever paid for, my lovely Victoria!" Lord Belvedere regarded Violet with satisfaction as he reclined in all his youthful glory upon the pink satin counterpane of the iron four-poster.

"It's Violet, actually," Violet said, pulling the bedsheets up to her chest as she swung her legs over the edge of the bed.

Through the thin walls of Madame Chambon's infamous house of assignation sounded the thumps and cries of the night's trade. Strange that this had become normal to her now, she thought as she began to untangle her long dark hair with her fingers. Strange, too, the way she'd experienced real excitement from the moment the young nobleman had gazed into her eyes before kissing her. And then doing all those other things that constituted bedroom sport.

"Actually, it's the first tupping I *have* ever paid for—and worth every penny, my exquisite Violet." Belvedere grinned as he met her look, then reached forward to draw her back down beside him. "Where *did* you learn those tricks?"

"I could ask you the same, my Lord," Violet replied, gently disengaging herself from his embrace so she could return to her task of ordering herself. For once, it was more than lip service. It *was* the best tupping of this strange, sordid year.

It was also the first time she'd felt regret at cutting short a business encounter; something she'd have to do if she wasn't to anger her most reliable and high-paying customer, Lord Bainbridge. He'd probably be pacing the length of the drawing room downstairs like a caged tiger by now.

With an extremely satisfied sigh, Lord Belvedere put his hands behind his head and crossed his ankles. "And I would answer that pleasing a woman has always been a favourite pursuit of mine." He continued to regard Violet with appreciation. "Now, surely I can persuade you to finish our delightful encounter with less unseemly haste. Let's order a bottle of champagne and bring out the draughts board, shall we?"

Violet flicked a quick glance at him as she leaned over to roll on one of the fine, white stockings she'd hung over the iron bed end. He really was rather a delicious specimen with his soulful caramel eyes. And that beautifully curved mouth was as accomplished at kissing as it was issuing quips that made her laugh. This last hour they'd done all that and more as they'd rolled about on the counterpane in Violet's attic room, with its view of St Paul's being its most redeeming feature. There weren't many other redeeming features at Madame Chambon's.

Lord Belvedere looked in no hurry to leave. He stretched languidly, and Violet tried to hide her interest in assessing his unashamedly naked form. She'd never felt anything, other than revulsion, for any of the men she entertained in order to keep a roof over her head. Until now.

"Yes, champagne and draughts is just the thing, I say!" He

sat up, clicking his fingers as he joined her on the edge of the bed, their naked thighs touching before Violet pulled her chemise over her head.

"I'm afraid no one is going to come running at your summons, my Lord." With a dampening smile, she turned and presented him with her back, holding up the long laces of her corset in a clear implication that she needed his help. "Regrettably, our time together is at an end, and I'd appreciate it if you helped make me decent. I presume you have done this before?"

"Naturally." But instead of the tug of laces, she felt his arms go over her shoulders to fondle her breasts while he pulled her against him and nuzzled her ear. She could feel the swell of his erection against her behind while the whisper of his breath against her ear stirred her insides into an unexpected state of anticipation.

The acknowledgement of this sensation of physical enjoyment was troubling.

"Nevertheless, I have no intention of leaving before we've ended matters in a civilised fashion." He kissed her shoulder and turned her to face him. "I realise there are men who consider it civilised, or within their rights, to pay an unseemly amount for sex and then leave the moment they come." He smiled pleasantly at her as he stroked her cheek. "I, however, am a gentleman, and I like to reward good value. You, my dear Violet, have given excellent value."

Violet blinked, surprised at the pang of regret she felt at his impending departure until she remembered how important the no doubt hideously impatient Lord Bainbridge was to her long-term goal of escaping Madame Chambon's house of assignation. Or bordello, nunnery, brothel, or whatever term it went by in the lexicon of the gentlemen who crossed its threshold in pursuit of London's most sought-after companions. Ladies of the night. Lightskirts. Fair Cyprians. She'd been called many things, but she rather liked the way 'my fair Violet' rolled off young Lord Belvedere's tongue. Just as she'd liked what young Lord Belvedere's tongue had done to her in a myriad of other unexpectedly erotic ways this evening.

"Madame Chambon will be most pleased," Violet murmured, extricating herself from his grasp.

"I have no interest in pleasing Madame Chambon."

It seemed Lord Belvedere was not going to be easily persuaded to leave. He cupped Violet's chin, turning her head slightly so that she was forced to look at him. "If I'm cutting into the time of your next highly anticipated customer, then perhaps Madame Chambon will be pleased if I double your rate just so we can drink champagne and play draughts together for half an hour. I trust you can play draughts? It's hardly a complicated game."

Violet considered him. She made no secret of it as her eyes roamed the length of him: his long, muscled thighs lightly dusted with the dark hair from which his manhood sprouted; further up, his well-delineated chest with its delicate nipples suggesting the first possibility of vulnerability. His mouth was the second. And it really was a lovely mouth, his lips soft though his jaw determined; as determined as his eyes as he stared back at her.

He indicated the bell that sat on her side table. "Surely you need only to ring that and a servant *will* come running to do our bidding?"

It was true. If Violet were creative enough, her next customer would be given the necessary excuse that would see him offered any of the other exceptional young women for whom Madame Chambon's establishment was renowned.

"Unless you would, in fact, prefer to be entertained by your next customer rather than drink champagne with me?" His voice was lower by several notches. Caramel and persuasive. Like his eyes.

No, Violet had no desire to entertain Lord Bainbridge but nor did she want to anger him. Lord Bainbridge was well on the way to making her that offer of exclusivity which every girl at Madame's craved.

She licked her lips as she stared back at his lordship. She'd happily drink champagne with him. Heavens! She'd happily roll about on the bed with him for another session, which was unheard of.

Violet contemplated her options. Perhaps denying Lord Bainbridge tonight might be just the ticket for hustling him along the road to setting her up in her own little ladybird's lair so Violet could shed this hated life and plan her next elevation.

Without a word, she picked up the little bell and sent the message for which his lordship was so eager. Champagne and a board game. What a perfectly delightful way to end an evening.

"Clever move, lovely Violet. You're as inspiring on the draughts board as you are in bed."

Predictably, they were once again back on the coverlet, Lord Belvedere stark naked, Violet in only a peignoir, but he'd been true to his expressed desires. It seemed he really did want to end their session with some rivalry on the draughts board and some lively conversation rather than once again demonstrating his prowess as a lover.

Violet watched his lordship toss back his champagne. His

cheeks were flushed and there was an air of excitement about him, or suppressed emotion, that she'd not noticed before.

With a gusty sigh, he set down his glass and sent Violet a long and level look as he leant back against the pillows. "Definitely a moment to celebrate. A lucky escape, if ever there was one."

Violet shook her head when he reached for the bottle on the bedside drawers and tried to top up her glass. "And what have you escaped, my Lord? A marauding tiger? The firing squad?" She tried to sound relaxed as she ran her forefinger over the smooth surface of the white piece she was waiting to move once it was her turn. She could see an opportunity that she suspected he'd missed.

"Not quite, though, either way, my fate would have been equally unhappy." Lord Belvedere leaned over, picked up his black, and neatly moved to take three of her pieces. "You thought I'd missed that, my love. But I'm not so stupid. Nor are you, for that matter." Then, in a more robust tone, "I was to have been married tonight. Can you believe it, but three hours ago I was all dressed up and standing at the altar in my very finest."

"You were to have been…married?" Violet felt her first flush of panic for the evening as she tried to discern if the beautiful…*naked*…man before her was in earnest.

If he was, then—what had she done?

Sensing her discomfort, he patted her wrist. "I waited at the altar for more than an hour for the wretched female." For the first time this evening he looked grim. "Lord, I certainly had everyone's sympathy by the time we all realised the game was over."

"I'm sorry." Violet plucked at the silken folds of her peignoir and thought how strangely different men were from women when dealing with crises of the heart.

Recalling the moment of realisation that the man she'd loved had let her down so terribly still sent ice through her veins, nearly two years later. But her first recourse had hardly been sexual diversion. A wave of self-revulsion engulfed her. Oh no, that had come much later. Though hardly at her behest.

"Lord, you can't imagine it! I'd arrived at the church feeling sick to my stomach with nerves but determined to do the right thing."

She searched for any sign of remorse on Lord Belvedere's part for having assuaged his wounded pride in the arms of a…lightskirt—oh, how she did suffer at the term that indicated how far she'd fallen.

But she could find none.

He glanced at her, then looked away, stroking the glossy tops of the marble pieces as he added, reflectively, "Of course, I got what I deserved. The whole debacle was, after all, my fault."

"What was your fault? That she didn't arrive?" Violet tried to imagine what scenario might have prevented an eager bride-to-be from making such an important appointment. Her self-recrimination of a moment before was replaced by a surge of anger towards the man in front of her. Somehow, she suspected, Lord Belvedere had evaded a marriage he didn't want. Perhaps he hadn't waited long enough. Perhaps he'd ensured his bride-to-be was detained on purpose. Oh, Violet knew of many underhand ways a man could slip and slide out of his obligations.

Yet, was she any better? If she were made of sterner stuff and lived by her principles, she'd point at the door and tell him to get out right now. No young woman should ever have to go through what Violet had gone through.

Just as quickly, the emotion drained away. Why should she expect any better from a client? Clearly Lord Belvedere, for all his charm and winning ways, was as morally deficient as all the rest.

And besides, one only had to see how far Violet had fallen than to know that she was the last person alive who could criticize another for their morals.

Lord Belvedere shook his head, unaware of her changed feelings towards him. "No, it was my fault for asking her to be there in the first place. For asking her to marry me when I knew she didn't want to. Standing there in the silent vestry, feeling the sympathy of the wedding guests while my own shame nearly felled me…well, it was just divine punishment." He took another sip, then kissed the tips of his fingers in a careless gesture of gallantry towards Violet.

Violet sought for a response. She was hardly about to exonerate him if that's what he wanted. "That sounds like an excuse to me. She wouldn't have accepted if she didn't want to marry you. What if she was in an accident and that's why she was delayed?" Her outrage grew. What a *terrible* thing for him to have done? Gone straight from the church to Violet's bed. Why, that made Violet implicit in causing an innocent young woman pain she did not deserve.

"Believe me, there was no accident. Mabel cried off at the last moment. She realised what I should have realised—that she should never have accepted me, and that she'd be making as big a mistake as I by trying to please our families rather than ourselves."

His face softened as he extended his arm and stroked Violet's shoulder. "No need to look like that. No harm done. Best thing that ever happened, in fact."

Violet frowned. She couldn't decide whether his cavalier attitude hid a broken heart, or whether he really was as over-joyed to be free as he made out.

"Your father must have been dismayed to say the least."

"Pater's been dead a long while. Mother the same. No trouble from that quarter." His smile broadened.

"So…the poor young lady's decision to cry off has left everyone happy? What a strange state of affairs."

"Well, not everyone was happy. My grandfather was irate, to say the least, as was hers. They share adjoining estates and thought the idea of forging the next generation to create a mighty union a capital idea." Lord Belvedere sighed and, for the first time, looked regretful as he toyed with the pieces. "My great-aunt, alas, is inconsolable."

Violet wasn't sure how to navigate such strange territory. "I suppose it's better if one doesn't get married just to please one's grandfather…or great-aunt," she said slowly while also thinking of the many women who married to please everyone in their families other than themselves.

Suddenly, he became brisk. "Now, where were we? Your turn, I believe?"

Violet studied the draughts board and made her move.

"Got me! And I didn't see it coming!" Lord Belvedere took another slug of champagne.

"That's either because you wanted to redeem yourself by playing the gentleman and letting me win or because your wits are addled."

He laughed as he moved one of his pieces three places. "I like to think of myself as a gentleman. I've not found myself in an establishment like this before. And as to my wits being addled, it is not, in fact, a sensation with which I'm terribly familiar. I like operating with a clear mind. Tonight is an exception."

"That would make you an anomaly amongst your set." Violet sent him a wicked smile across the top of her glass as he raised one eyebrow and clearly pondered a response. She wondered if he were the kind who was quick to anger when their manliness or any other apparent prowess was questioned, despite his assertions that suggested the contrary.

"I *am* an anomaly amongst my set apparently." He gestured to his surroundings with a sweep of his arm. "Yes, it's my first visit to a place like this, and I don't know why I allowed Bletchley—that's my best man—to persuade me to come here, though when I set eyes on you all objections died on my lips. But, do you know; I recognised three gentlemen. Married men, too." He shook his head. "Now, coming to a place like this when one is married is not, in my opinion, the mark of a gentleman."

Violet shifted position, uncomfortable with his talk. "Some of these men do not enjoy the comforts of home that they—"

"Feel entitled to?" he interrupted. He shook his head, his expression uncompromising. "Sorry, but that doesn't wash with me. They should have been wiser in their choice of wife."

"You do not recognise a double standard? I hardly believe you are practising as you preach, Lord Belvedere. Sorry if I sound sceptical, but don't you think you'd have soon been back through those doors to see me as a married man if the woman you wed proved unsatisfactory in bed?"

He sent her a level look and shook his head. "No."

"No?" Violet tried for her most artful smile in an attempt to lighten the mood.

To her surprise, he remained serious. "No. Honour and freedom are the codes by which I live. I was ready to follow the honourable path and do what Grandfather wished of me for the sake of the family. I'd have accepted my responsibility and I'd have been faithful, regardless of what it cost me. But when Mabel bolted, I was overwhelmed by the prospect of being, suddenly and unexpectedly, free." He relaxed, his beautiful smile transforming him into the most handsome man Violet thought she'd ever seen.

"My, but I am glad it was you who came to my rescue, sweet Violet. So much so that I'm truly sorry to leave you, knowing that I shan't be back."

A pang of regret ripped through her. Violet couldn't believe it. She actually wanted to welcome this man back into her arms and would have no issue telling him so? What's more, she'd mean it, for while she'd said similar words to Lord Bainbridge, that had been paying her most valuable customer the necessary lip service. Survival talk.

"You'd be very welcome," she said softly. And he would. In all the time she'd been at Madame Chambon's, Violet had never met a man as charming as Lord Belvedere.

"Ah well." He began to neaten the draughts board, placing the scattered pieces in their rightful places. Violet couldn't keep her eyes off his hands. They were long-fingered and gentle. Well, gentle when needed, and very successful in whipping up her long-dormant sexual impulses, too. She swallowed, hoping he didn't notice the blush that brightened her cheeks as she recalled the clearly mutually enjoyable exploits that had so recently played out upon her bed.

He looked up. "Lightskirts are forbidden in my code of gallantry, and tonight will be a single lapse before I pick myself up after the tumultuous events of this afternoon and forge ahead as the gentleman I propose to be."

Violet ignored the taunt to her calling. "I think you are more upset about being jilted than you would allow."

"My pride was dented, it's true, but I am more excited about the freedom ahead of me than I am downcast at losing face."

Violet held out her empty glass, then raised it in a toast as the foaming liquid spilled over the edge. "Here's to your freedom, my Lord. Go forth and make the most of it for not many of us know what freedom is."

He raised his eyebrows as if her words surprised him, stopping with the glass poised at his lips. "And what is freedom for you, my lovely Violet?"

"Choosing the man upon whom I bestow my favours." She regretted the words the moment they were out and hoped one of Madame's spies didn't have their ear to the wall. Gentlemen paid a fortune to come to this house in order to feel they were the centre of the universe.

"Ah, so that's why you're so pleased I'm here since you invited me back, and it's clear we like one another." In one swift movement, he placed his glass upon the chest of drawers and pushed her back onto the mattress, kissing her thoroughly on the mouth while one hand skimmed her thigh.

To Violet's astonishment, her body responded with a skittering of pleasurable anticipation right the way up her spine while her womb pulsed with desire.

Until, to her equal surprise, her pleasure was replaced by a sense of desolation when he rolled off her and stood up, casting about for his shirt which he began pulling over his head.

"You have been utterly beguiling, my delicious Violet," he said, as his head emerged and he positioned his stiffened collar before reaching for his trousers. His light-brown eyes sparkled. He truly did look like a man who was both satisfied yet regretful to be leaving.

But surely he'd come back?

"And, dear girl, you deserve all the freedom you desire."

"So, freedom for you is simply not being married to Miss Mabel?" Violet couldn't let him go without knowing more. "Is that all?"

"Freedom for me is adventuring across the seas to foreign

lands. I was supposed to be heading off on my wedding tour to the Continent as we speak, but I've a notion that Africa will suit me far better." As he worked to slide his cufflinks into place, his expression took on a faraway look. "Yes, Africa. There's gold and diamonds to be discovered there. Perhaps I'll book my passage to Cape Town the moment I step out of here. I could invest in a gold mine. And shoot some lions and tigers. After all, I'm a free man now without obligations for the very first time I can remember. I can do anything I want. You have no idea how wonderful it is to say those words out loud, Violet. *I'm free.*"

Violet watched him in silence. Already he was leaping forward in his life, envisioning all the marvellous opportunities that stretched ahead. She felt like weeping at the vast chasm between what each could hope for from their respective futures. Instead, she murmured, "There are no tigers in Africa."

He stopped as he slid the second cufflink home, his lips trembling with suppressed amusement. "Not only beautiful, you are also clever, Violet. I was testing you, of course. Though what would you know about tigers?"

The pounding in her head made her close her eyes. *What would she know about tigers?* More than he'd ever find out, she thought painfully.

"A little," she ventured. But he was too occupied with tidying himself to attend to her properly. Finally satisfied with his appearance, he turned and put his hands on her shoulders.

"Farewell, my lovely Violet. Thank you for this evening. You brought me back from the brink."

"But now you will never think of me again. Or visit?"

Why had she said that? It sounded bitter, and that was something she'd sworn she would never be. Not like her grandmother who revelled in it, and who'd ensured the orphans thrust upon her would never know what it was like to be carefree as their punishment for being born.

He was halfway to the door but he turned, a myriad of emotions flitting across his face. What a handsome man he was, his well-cut suit highlighting his broad shoulders and long legs, his smile boyish and heartrending. In two strides, he returned to sweep her into his arms and kissed her deeply.

A long, languid, thorough kiss that left her shaking and desperate for more when they both came up for air.

For a moment, they remained clasped tightly in one another's arms, the only sound their heavy breathing.

After a moment, he whispered, "No, I will not return, alas. But I've enjoyed what we shared." He held her away from him and gently touched her lips with his forefinger. "It was a…particularly satisfying intimacy I could never engage in with a young lady I'd only just met."

"You just did."

"With a marriage prospect, then." He cleared his throat and seemed to try for a brisker, more lighthearted tone. "Well now, my *clever* Violet who possesses such attention to detail, it has been an absolute pleasure meeting you." He dropped his hands and made for the door. "I wish you all the best for your life. You never know, perhaps I'll send a postcard from the Sudan or Cairo, for I don't expect I'll forget you in a hurry."

"Please address it to Miss Violet Lilywhite," Violet murmured, wanting to imprint it on his brain. "And you can always ask for me by name if you can toss out your scruples and step over Madame's threshold. Remember, it's *Violet*, not Victoria. Violet like the colour of the sunsets you dream of experiencing on the dark continent and Lilywhite because," she touched her heart, "though my soul may seem black with sin to you, now, it was lily white when I stumbled into this house."

A shadow flickered across his face. He looked about to question her. Then he smiled; genuine and regretful as he put his hand on the doorknob. "I'm afraid I shan't be back, but I shall certainly relive this lovely evening with you when I recline in my chair in the heart of the African bush and gaze at the setting sun. And I'll certainly recommend you to the more discerning of my set. Decent fellows, they are. Because a girl like you deserves the best."

CHAPTER 2

When Max stalked into the breakfast parlour at ten o'clock, feeling distinctly jaded following his exploits of the night before, he was dismayed to find it occupied.

"Rather late for you to be breakfasting, Aunt Euphemia," he remarked, for she generally rose at six and liked to eat shortly afterwards.

"I'm not such a creature of habit," the old lady said with a clearly fabricated attempt at artlessness. Max knew she'd been doggedly sitting here for hours just so she could waylay him. As of course she'd feel obliged to do.

Not that he intended calling her out on it.

Or indulging her desire for revisiting yesterday's events.

After helping himself to haddock and eggs from the side-board, he took a seat opposite her then pulled the newspaper towards him before hesitating. Did he really have the forti-tude to see his public shame laid out in newsprint for the world to see? No doubt Aunt Euphemia had read the article three times.

"I don't think you should read it, Max," she said, dabbing

her eyes with her lace handkerchief before stifling a little cough she was soon unable to control.

A fortuitous interruption which might deflect her entirely from mentioning that which Max intended never to mention again. His marriage. Before, present, or future. He'd dodged a bullet and he was off to Africa to celebrate.

"I wonder if you're well enough to be up and about, Aunt," he said, frowning. "Has grandfather not called the doctor?"

"I've been consulting doctors for months and there's nothing a doctor can do for me now, Max." Her tone of resignation made him glance up from his food.

"What do you mean, Aunt?"

She didn't meet his eye, but he studied her as she daintily tore a croissant in half. Her fingers had always been birdlike, but he observed for the first time that the rest of her was distinctly more birdlike than he remembered. Aunt Euphemia had never been a robust figure of health, but she'd dished out justice and hugs with the necessary strength to satisfy a young orphan boy who'd craved both.

"We all must go sometime, Max."

He felt unaccountably panicked as he searched her face for refutation of that which she'd implied. "You're far from old, Aunt Euphemia." He didn't know if he should grip her hand or what he should say. "You've caught a chill. We all suffer from inflammation of the lungs but you're taking a little longer to get better this time."

Knowing that the sadness in her smile was sympathy for him and not self-pity doubled his pain. Watching her distress as another hacking cough gripped her was unbearable.

"I'd have liked longer but there it is," she managed, dabbing at her mouth. She looked so frail in the harsh sunlight that filtered through the window that Max felt like leaping up and enfolding her in his arms. The buttered toast he tried to swallow tasted like ashes.

"I had so hoped to see you settled and happy."

Max nearly said that the two certainly did not go together where he was concerned but thought better of it. Aunt Euphemia had always been such a hopeless romantic, and if it gave her pleasure to believe Max was like any normal, red-blooded young man who aspired to marrying the 'right' girl, he'd do it.

"I don't know what possessed Mabel to do what she did. That letter she sent you made no sense at all."

Max grunted. He'd received Mabel's hastily scrawled missive when he'd arrived back from Madame Chambon's, but by that stage was so buoyed up by spirits—whisky and euphoria from the wonderful time he'd had with that damned fine barque of frailty he'd met there—to care a jot for Mabel's reasons for crying off.

She'd said she simply didn't love him as he deserved to be loved, so what was good for the goose should be good for the gander. Clearly, romantic love was more important to Mabel than Max had understood, in which case she deserved better than be bound to him for life.

Aunt Euphemia coughed delicately. "You'd have been a good husband, Max. Kind. Considerate. There are few enough men who fall into that category. Mabel has made a grave error, and I only pray she'll come to her senses before I'm in my grave."

"Aunt, please don't talk like that. It was for the best!" Max reached across and patted her hand, conscious of its papery feel, tempering the alarm in his tone. The thought of not having Aunt Euphemia to come home to once he'd sown his wild oats and returned to familial duty left him bereft.

He cleared his throat. "To tell you the truth, I couldn't be more relieved." If only to lessen her pain, he had to reassure her that he was not brokenhearted. Which he wasn't. He'd been piqued and embarrassed but that had quickly given way to relief. As for his grandfather, let him believe what he liked. Max felt no sense of responsibility for pleasing the old man who'd criticised Max his whole life.

But Aunt Euphemia was in a different category. Max would do anything to make her happy. He began to stroke her hand, smiling to try and erase the sadness from her eyes.

"Oh, you say it, Max, but what will you do now? You and Mabel were to be married after having known each other for so very many years. A whole wonderful world of family and domesticity has been snatched from you by her cruel and selfish behaviour of yesterday."

Max laughed softly. If only his aunt knew how desperately Max had railed against the notion of family and domesticity. As his marriage had drawn closer, he'd felt increasingly trapped and desperate.

But that's not what his aunt wanted to hear. She'd spent most of her adult life in mourning for the one true love her brother had refused to allow her.

He gently chafed the backs of her hands from across the breakfast table. "I'd only admit it to you, Aunt Euphemia, but I wasn't in love with Mabel, nor she with me. We were doing what our grandfathers wanted rather than following our own hearts. But Mabel was braver than me. She cried off and I applaud her for it."

"Oh no, Max!" Aunt Euphemia's mouth dropped open. "You've been childhood sweethearts for fifteen years."

"We've known each other as neighbours for fifteen years," Max corrected her. "And we were too young and ignorant to object when our grandfathers conceived the notion that we should become betrothed. I've never felt romantic love for Mabel nor she for me. She'll be much happier with some worthy and deserving husband who can lavish upon her the attention and compliments I never could. In fact, I'd not be surprised if she made such an announcement before the year was over."

"Mabel was in love with someone else?" His aunt gasped, pulling back her hands to put them to her face.

"I'm almost sure of it."

Aunt Euphemia's mouth trembled. "And what about you, Max? That's all very well for Mabel, but now you've been abandoned. You're all alone with no one to love yet you're in the prime of your life." She dropped her hands and raised her chin, her look determined. "I shall find you someone, Max. Before I go, and if it's the last thing I do, I will see you happily settled with a young woman who deserves you." She squared her shoulders, and an alarming note of enthusiasm crept into her voice as she continued, "The London season is just around the corner. I shall ensure you are invited to every event worth attending. Never mind that you've been embarrassed, I shall see that it's to your advantage—"

"Aunt, please... no!" Max had to stop her. This was the last thing he wanted. He was off to Africa, and there was an end to it. He'd intended booking his ticket this very day.

Cut off in midstride, his aunt blinked at him. "But Max, you're nearly twenty-six. You have family obligations. You must marry."

That might be sadly true, but his grandfather was still in good health and had no intention of handing over the reins to let Max manage the estate for a good number of years yet. This was the perfect opportunity for Max to run away to sea or to hunt lions or discover diamonds. His sudden and unexpected release yesterday from the shackles of matrimony had fired him up with renewed enthusiasm for life.

"But Aunt, I don't want to be dragged about London ballrooms and drawing rooms in search of a wife." He'd have to be honest or his aunt would find some way of altering his resolve. She might be frail, but Max knew he'd be dangerously susceptible to agreeing to a night out here and an event there, just because it would please her so much.

She pressed her lips together and blinked rapidly as if to stem the tears he could see glittering in her surprisingly clear blue eyes. His aunt had never been a beauty, but he could see how her sweet nature would have been appealing to the suitor she'd spoken of so wistfully over the years. The suitor her brother had sent packing because he didn't have the pocketbook or address Aunt Euphemia's older and exacting brother deemed worthy of the family.

"Don't run the danger of closing your heart off to sentiment just because of what happened yesterday," she said softly. "I may have been disappointed in love but let me tell you that it's the greatest emotion a person can feel." She pressed a trembling hand to her breast. "I would not go to my grave without the knowledge that you've been touched by it too, my boy." She took a shuddering breath. "You're the closest to a son I've had, and you lost your darling mother—and your father—much too young. All your life you've been looking for love, Max. Don't start pretending to me, now, that you don't need it."

"Please, Aunt, that's not what I'm saying at all." Max was feeling rather desperate and beleaguered right now. "I simply said I didn't want to be paraded all about London in search of a wife."

"And I'll not go to my grave knowing you are lonely and still looking for love, Max."

"But you won't. I mean, you're not going to your grave for a good long time, besides." He looked down, buttering another piece of toast he didn't think he could eat.

"It's what the doctor says, Max, and there's the truth. Another winter as cold as the last will see the end of me. That's why I need to put my affairs in order. Doctor's orders."

She sounded more resolute and accepting than Max could have imagined anyone would be following such a dire pronouncement.

He swallowed. Not his toast, but the lump in his throat. "Then the last thing you need is to squire me around—if that's the right term—in the hopes of hitching me up with some worthy female before season's end."

"It is the very thing I need," she said stolidly.

"But…but pointless," Max responded, flailing as he found himself unable to drag his gaze away from her gimlet eye. "Pointless because…because my heart is already engaged to another."

"Oh, Max! Why didn't you say? So it's not only Mabel whose affections have been engaged elsewhere?"

Max hesitated. The way her face lit up at the thought that romance might be in the air gave him a jolt of pleasure. But only momentarily. This was one lie he'd have to extricate himself from, so he'd better not get himself in too deep at the outset.

"Penniless, unfortunately. Totally unsuitable. Grandfather would never countenance it. No more to be said, really." He began to chew, his thoughts in turmoil, hoping his aunt would be satisfied.

Of course, she was not.

"Is she beautiful? She must be if she has nothing else to recommend her. Oh Max, do describe her to me."

Max sighed and lifted his teacup to his mouth while he sought for inspiration. "Well, she has milky-white skin," he began slowly, "and very dark hair and a glorious smile. Oh, and her eyes. Just like sapphires. I know it's a cliché, but they really are." He was talking more rapidly now as he warmed to his theme. Really, it was quite easy to paint a picture of a fictional love interest when he could base it on someone real. "She's quite unaffected in the way most young ladies are. No simpering, saying things just to please a man. That sort of thing, if you understand me."

"She sounds very…direct. But penniless, you say. What does her father do?"

Max pursed his lips. He had no idea, of course, though he must have been a complete reprobate or possibly even unknown considering his daughter did what she did for a living. Not that Max could tell his aunt what the lady he most admired did for a living.

"What does her father do?" he repeated slowly, while his brain raced to come up with something plausible. "Why, he's dead. That's why his daughter has to—"

"Good lord! The poor girl has to work? Is that what you're saying? That you've fallen in love with a…a serving girl?"

"Not a serving girl, Aunt. No, a… working girl. I mean a shop girl." Yes, that could just about pass muster.

"And what's her name?"

"Violet." That was easy though he was surprised the name came out so readily. The name that matched the description he'd just given Aunt Euphemia.

"You've fallen in love with a *shop girl*, Max?"

Max feigned regret, unable to meet his aunt's eyes in case she called him out on his lie and insisted again on trailing him through a dozen London drawing rooms. She'd really do it, he feared. And he'd not be able to say no to her.

"I have. Grandfather would be appalled, which is why, naturally, I've kept it very close. But…" he looked appealingly at Aunt Euphemia, 'that is the reason why of course I have no heart for society. My love for Violet is impossible, I realise, yet I can muster no enthusiasm at this present time for pursuing other, more suitable, potential brides." He touched his heart and mustered a sad, sympathetic smile for his aunt's benefit. "Surely you, of all people, understand this, Aunt Euphemia."

Aunt Euphemia reached out a trembling hand though her grip upon his wrist was surprisingly strong.

"Yes, Max. I, of *all* people, understand."

"And you'll speak no word of it to grandfather?"

Her fingers clenched at the mention of the brother Max knew she detested. They were of one accord in this, at least. Lord Granville had shown little kindness to either of them in his nearly seventy years.

"You have my word, Max."

Max nodded, his expression serious. "Thank you, Aunt Euphemia." With relief, he rose, his unsatisfactory breakfast heavy in his stomach, yet the moment he could make his escape through those parlour doors he'd feel a new lightness; he knew.

"You're a brick; you know that?" He grinned, his heart lifting at the sight of her smile. The moment he was out of those doors he'd make enquiries of Aunt Euphemia's doctor as to just what the problem was regarding that cough. Surely it was nothing that a winter in Spain couldn't fix. He'd hire a reliable travelling companion so she could escape London's harsh and miserable upcoming winter.

In the meantime though, he was off to book his passage on the first suitable vessel to Cape Town.

By the time he passed through the doors of the breakfast parlour he did, indeed, feel a hundred pounds lighter.

As if his life was only now about to begin.

CHAPTER 3

*V*iolet lay on her bed watching the shadows dancing on the walls as the sun that seeped through her thin curtains grew weaker.

She was exhausted and not relishing the prospects of what the night ahead might bring. More disappointment. More affirmation that her life was meaningless. How ironic that she could debase herself so much for the sake of dignity.

"Come in," she called at the sound of a light knock on the door. It would be Daisy asking why she wasn't in the drawing room with the other girls.

And, indeed, it was Daisy but holding a crisp cream envelope, embossed, she saw a moment later, causing her heart to lurch. The only person who would address a letter to her on such fine notepaper certainly did not have her best interests at heart.

She waited for Daisy to leave before she tore it open roughly. Although no longer did she have the niceties to hand like the silver letter opener her mother used for the invitations she used to receive, the letter hardly deserved to be treated nicely. The handwriting was unfamiliar but had no doubt been dictated.

"Dear Miss Lilywhite..." it began.

Yes, it had been dictated, and by someone of exceptional politeness in that the salutation was followed by an apology for the gross lack of manners in being so forward in addressing her with no prior introduction, but that skulduggery of such a nature required a little forgiveness, especially when the sender was motivated by only the best of intentions.

That was rare in a place like this, Violet thought with a stab of irony, squinting in perplexity once she'd digested the contents of the missive before again being overcome by trepidation.

Meet at Claridge's at 4 o' clock, the writer, a Miss Euphemia Thistlethwaite had requested.

Who on earth was Miss Thistlethwaite? Quite likely respectable, if the notepaper and language were anything to go by. But what did she want of Violet? No doubt she was an emissary who was being well rewarded for her work. Why else would a respectable woman wish to meet with Violet. Be *seen* with Violet, for that matter. And, in Claridge's, of all places.

Violet's first instinct was to pen a polite rebuttal for how could she possibly show her face in a restaurant patronised by London's wealthy and titled? What if she recognised someone? Or, worse, someone recognised her? Though that would be unlikely in a setting so different from the seamy world her clients patronised.

She pondered her options a moment before picking up a pen.

So what if recognition triggered mild confusion or even outright horror? It would hardly be to Violet's detriment.

A LITTLE LESS THAN FOUR HOURS LATER VIOLET, DRESSED demurely in a navy serge princess-line dress with white lace at her throat and cuffs, was led through the double doors of Claridge's restaurant and, having named the person she was to be joining, towards a table near the window.

As the personage was facing the street, Violet was given the benefit of sizing up her…adversary? Was Miss Thistlethwaite here to demand more of Violet than she'd already given? Though lord only knew there was little more Violet could give.

She felt suddenly ill and, to her disgust, realised it was with hope. Since Violet could be reviled no more than she currently was, she *could* only rise in the world. Perhaps her grandmother had chosen to forgive her on her deathbed? Perhaps Violet had come into some small legacy?

"Miss Thistlethwaite?" She tried to sound confident. As if she had as much right to dine at Claridge's as anyone else.

A pheasant's feather was nearly dislodged, as the owner of a romantically festooned piece of millinery turned a pair of smiling blue eyes upon Violet.

"Why, you are exactly what I was expecting," she exclaimed to Violet's confusion as she invited her to sit. "Though perhaps, even more of a beauty. But then, that's hardly surprising. Max always did appreciate beauty of the bolder variety."

"Max?"

"Your secret is out, my dear." The playful wag of Miss Thistlethwaite's fingers compounded Violet's horror.

"Max…told you about me?" But then, of course, this lady must be referring to a different Max. Not delicious Lord Belvedere from the previous night who'd said his name was

Max, and whom Violet must try not to think about again or she'd find all her other clients wanting.

"He most certainly did."

Violet let out a slow breath. Then this Max must have known Violet from long ago. From during the time a gentleman related to a lady like Miss Thistlethwaite would have been happy enough to have claimed an association with Violet.

The emotion conveyed by Violet's furrowed brow was, however, mistaken by Miss Thistlethwaite who, immediately upon ordering the sweets trolley to be brought round to their table, said, "Have no fear that I'll divulge any of this to his grandfather. Naturally, he's opposed to darling Max contracting a marriage to anyone less than an heiress, but since Max's happiness is all that matters, I am here to facilitate his happiness and, I trust, yours." She reached across the table, nearly touching Violet's gloved hand, before withdrawing it quickly, perhaps perceiving the inappropriateness of such familiarity on so little association. Clearly, Miss Thistlethwaite was a woman who acted on her heartstrings. Rather endearing really, Violet thought with a little tug of her own heartstrings. Her mother had been the same. Not Violet, though. Or Emily. They'd had to learn to guard their hearts when they could only trust one another.

Now, of course, Violet had no one. No one to trust, though she did like Miss Thistlethwaite with her bright, eager eyes and her birdlike movements. The elderly lady seemed like someone who really did believe that happiness could be plucked from thin air.

"If you are referring to the Max I believe you are, he was to have been wed to a worthy young lady only last night," Violet said slowly. Then, at Miss Thistlethwaite's nod, added, "A much more suitable young lady than I." For if Miss

Thistlethwaite supposed Violet could possibly be a marital contender, then it would be far better to nip such delusions in the bud before anyone was more embarrassed than they need be.

"Indeed he was. Jilted at the altar. Terrible business! Why, I thought his heart was breaking until I realised it had already been broken." She pointed an accusing finger at Violet. "By you, Miss Lilywhite. Yes, no need to look so concerned. I've already told you I've no intention of divulging this to anyone. Not before the time is right."

"When the time is right?' Violet clasped her hands together in her lap to stop them shaking while she thought of gorgeous young Max. Of his strong, muscled young body, his dazzling smile and his…

She closed her eyes. She must not think of that when she was speaking to his aunt, though the athleticism with which he'd conducted himself still had Violet's body in thrall.

"Miss Thistlethwaite, you…you don't know what kind of girl I am." She swallowed. There really would be too much embarrassment to follow any wild assumptions on Miss Thistlethwaite's part being allowed to flourish. "I don't know what Max has said about me, but he surely hasn't hinted at what you seem to think." She couldn't even put it into words. Marriage? Violet would be lucky to marry one of the burly protectors who lounged about Madame Chambon's premises to keep the girls safe. More likely, though, she'd be discarded the moment her looks started to fade. Not every girl was as lucky as Charity whose devoted young man paid a small fortune to Madame Chambon to protect the girl he'd met the night they'd both shed their virginity, and whom he was determined to wed when he came into his inheritance in a year's time.

"Not to you, perhaps. He was, after all, acceding to duty

by wedding his childhood friend until she cried off." Miss Thistlethwaite looked overjoyed. "But now he's free." She dabbed at her eyes. "You're both free. When Max told me he'd long been in love with a young lady with absolutely nothing other than her charm and beauty to recommend her, I resolved there and then that I would ensure I would go to my grave knowing my darling Max could marry the woman he truly loved."

Violet's mouth felt very dry. She took a sip of the water that had just been placed in front of her and managed, "I think you have rather jumped to conclusions, Miss Thistlethwaite."

"Oh, no need to keep playing the game for my benefit. I see how it is." The woman's eyes twinkled. "You both knew Lord Granville would disapprove—as he would, no doubt about it—if you and Max were to marry. But I know what it is to live one's whole life with the disappointment of being denied one's true love purely on account of lack of finances, and I'm determined that is not going to happen to Max."

Violet frowned. "I'm sure I can't imagine what Max said about me," she fished. "Or how you even knew where to find me."

Miss Thistlethwaite wagged her finger playfully at Violet once again. "If I'd been born a man, I'd have become one of those special policemen or investigators searching for clues. I'm good at it. Sniffing out secrets. When it was clear Max didn't want to say any more about you—no doubt fearing I might unwisely tell his grandfather—I simply had John Coachman deliver my letter to the premises Max had visited the previous night. It was very simple, really."

Violet spluttered. "So *that's* how you found me?"

Unabashed by the sheer horror in Violet's tone, Miss Thistlethwaite put a sympathetic hand on Violet's arm.

"There'll be no shame in Max marrying as soon as he wishes, and I shall do all I can to facilitate it. You and Max can rely upon it. I've an independent fortune, you know, and if I want to spend it on a wedding trousseau for the bride of my favourite nephew, that's my decision to make."

CHAPTER 4

Max tried to focus through the haze of blue-tinged pipe smoke that blanketed the tavern. Loud, coarse voices and the chink of glass and pewter on countertop and table further dulled his senses. He'd had only a couple of brandies, but surely his eyes were deceiving him for it couldn't be possible that the young woman who'd just slipped into the booth opposite him was Miss Lilywhite.

Touting for business? That wasn't the way she operated, and surely not the way Madame Chambon's operated?

Not that he wasn't pleased. Thoroughly delighted was more apt, perhaps. His groin ached with want at the very sight of her, and he had to remind himself of his pledge to swear off loose women. Forever. Respectable, willing women were a different matter, and he'd availed himself of a number of those over the years at opportune times. Last night, however, was the first time he'd paid for the services of a prostitute, and he didn't intend doing so again.

"Miss Lilywhite, what a surprise," he said, beckoning to the barmaid, for the least he could do was offer her a drink. "How did you manage to hunt me down here?"

Max cast his very interested gaze the length of what he could see. Miss Lilywhite was dressed more like one of these new office workers in her dark-blue woollen skirt and white blouse with its demure collar and cuffs, her rich brown hair simply coiffured with one ringlet falling over her shoulder from beneath her pert blue hat. Nothing like the siren he remembered. Although a woman in a place like this was unusual, no one would give either of them a second glance and yet, last night, writhing in a pool of lust and sweat as he'd exorcised himself of the need for sexual release, she'd been the siren of his dreams. Exquisite face. Soft, white, voluptuous body. Inventive repertoire.

He smiled his admiration. "I must say, I simply would not have recognised you."

"I hardly imagine you would have. A woman like me needs to know how to dress and behave if she's to get on in life. As to hunting you down, I've shown no more ingenuity there than your aunt with whom I've just dined at Claridge's. I paid a boy a few coins to tell me where to find you."

"Good God! My aunt surely didn't find you at—"

"Don't worry; she doesn't know where I live, and she doesn't know what I am. Tea was very pleasant, and her blissful ignorance remains intact." Miss Lilywhite smiled serenely at his horror. "However, I did feel it important to let you know that she is labouring under the misconception that you are madly in love with me and wish to marry me. Apparently, it is her greatest wish that she facilitates this, despite the fact I am clearly only a..."

Max waited, and saw she was enjoying drawing out the suspense of what his aunt actually believed Miss Lilywhite to be. "A poor shop girl fallen on hard times with a respectable enough family. I think your grandfather's expected opposition might have fuelled her enthusiasm."

"I'm impressed at your perception, Miss Lilywhite—and

for taking the trouble to inform me." He felt at a bit of a loss here and was glad of the interruption of the waitress who'd just set down another brandy for Max and a cider for his companion.

"Naturally, I have no expectations of becoming your bride, Lord Belvedere, or even further association with you," she said smoothly, her smile indicating her amusement at his momentary loss of composure. "Your aunt is a charming woman; I liked her immensely! And she has only your best interests at heart. I'd certainly not see her disappointed, so I merely thought it best to let you know that whatever you've inadvertently said to give her such a false impression should be rectified." Her smile broadened as she raised her glass. "I'm curious, though. How did my name come up in conversation between you and your aunt?"

Max grinned. "Not through anything pertaining to the truth, I can tell you that much. No, I was trying to deflect her from finding me an alternative bride by pulling up the first name that came to mind, and telling her I'd been madly in love with this woman but realised the impossibility of a union which is why I'm off to Africa in three weeks."

"I do hope you'll make a return visit to Madame Chambon's establishment before you go."

Max felt truly regretful as he shook his head. "I've sworn off—" He stopped himself in time, but she took no offence, merely threw back her head so that her lovely, swanlike neck was more in evidence and laughed. The image was such a modest and charming re-creation of last night's spectacular sexual gymnastics that he felt himself heating from head to toe all over again.

"You've sworn off immoral women like me, have you? Well, that's a different discussion." Miss Lilywhite didn't seem the slightest bit put out by his less than gentlemanly insinuation as to the type of woman he considered her. "But what do you intend telling your aunt in order to rectify this problem? I don't want her landing on Madame Chambon's doorstep and being exposed to loose, immoral women. It would be distressing to her, to you, *and* to me." She put her head on one side, and in that moment, Max thought her the most beautiful creature he'd ever laid eyes on. Her skin was like alabaster. He'd thought it last night as he'd run his hands over its nakedness, and he thought it now in the coarsest of daytime situations. Her eyes were like two glittering sapphires. What he admired as much, though, was her vivacity and her lovely humour. Not to mention her compassion. Anyone who showed such consideration towards his beloved aunt was a thoroughly good person.

Thoughtfully, he ran his fingers across his lower lip, not realising for a few seconds that he was yet again reliving last night when she'd done the same to him. And how much he'd liked it!

"You're a good actress, you say, Miss Lilywhite? Were you acting last night?"

"What?"

"Acting? When you were in bed with me? Surely you haven't forgotten already?"

To his amusement, she blushed. Sudden and fiery as she glanced at the noisy table beside them rather than meet his eye, though she didn't seem embarrassed when she returned her gaze to his face.

"Last night is not what is under discussion; however, in the interests of telling the truth, which I like to do whenever it is at all possible—since, so often, it is not—I thought you the most exciting and desirable of any gentleman who has ever crossed my threshold, and I'm deeply regretful that this is the last time we shall meet. Now, what *is* under discussion is what you wish me to say in order to cause the least distress possible to a charming old lady who is clearly very innocent, unworldly, and wants only the best for her favourite nephew." She clasped her gloved hands upon the table and smiled at Max, who was feeling unaccountably churned up by her earlier revelation so that he was barely attending when she added, slowly, as if he were a simpleton, "What do you want me to say to Miss Thistlethwaite if she contacts me again?" Then, even more slowly as he still hadn't found the right response, "Please attend to me, Lord Belvedere. I shan't see you again and I promise not to follow you, so now is your only opportunity to ensure I do my part to curb your aunt's wild flight of fancy. We need to ensure our stories align."

Max blinked. Her words had had a very odd effect on him, as if he were opening himself up to a world of impoverishment if he didn't see her at least one more time. She really was quite captivating.

"You're very impatient for an answer, Miss Lilywhite, considering this has all come as rather a shock, and fellows like me are not known for making their greatest romantic gestures under stress."

She sat back and took another sip of cider. "I'd hardly put this in that category, but I'll wait. I'm in no hurry to get back to Madame Chambon's. It's a rare afternoon off so I'm rather enjoying it with preferred company." Her lips turned up in that delightful, half-amused way that made his insides tingle with want. But he couldn't be rash about this. Of course he couldn't. He was off to Africa to fulfill his greatest desire now that he'd at last been granted his freedom.

"You might not put this in the category of a great romantic gesture, but I do. Aunt Euphemia's heart beats as passionately as it ever did, and *I'd* not be the one to disappoint her."

"So, you want *me* to cry off? To tell her I have no wish to marry you? That would end it cleanly, I suppose."

Oh no, he didn't want her to do that at all. It would finish the matter far too peremptorily, he realised, when he was having rather a lot of fun right now. So he was surprised at how pleased he was when she added, "Unfortunately, it would come across as rather odd for a mere shop girl to throw away such a material rise in fortune, not to mention being suddenly and completely at odds with the glowing terms I used to describe you only a few hours ago."

"Glowing terms? Oh, I do like the sound of that. Tell me what you said."

She tapped her forefinger thoughtfully on her glass. "You already have a healthy opinion of yourself, Lord Belvedere. And I've already bolstered it. I'm not sure I want to enlarge any further."

"What if I started by telling you that I think you are the most stunning creature I've ever had occasion to meet, and I'm disappointed that any further association with you would kibosh my lofty intentions towards virtue. Besides which, as I've mentioned, I won't be around too much longer." He flashed her his most winning smile for he truly was impatient to know how Miss Lilywhite had described him to his aunt.

"And is that the truth, Lord Belvedere?"

"I like to tell the truth when at all possible."

"As do I, as I've said. All right, I told her that I thought you the handsomest and most considerate of any gentleman who'd ever crossed my threshold—bearing in mind she thinks I work in a shop—and that I'd immediately lost my heart to you upon first sight." She looked a little embarrassed. "And that every time you walk into a room my heart beats as loudly as a drum, and I have to exercise all my self-restraint to continue whatever polite conversation I'm involved in so as not to rush across the room and kiss you thoroughly. Oh, she did enjoy that! I could see how much she wanted to hear you talked up to the stars and I really did gild the lily. You should have seen how pink she went and how delighted to find me as ardent an admirer of your virtues as herself."

"Kindred spirits, eh?" He grinned. "Miss Lilywhite, you said you like to tell the truth when possible. Tell me how much was merely embellishment for my aunt?"

"Very little, really. But I've already made it clear how much I like you. That's no secret. Nevertheless, we've strayed from the matter under discussion since it seems you only want your head turned. What. Should. I. Tell. Miss Thistlethwaite?"

"What should you tell Miss Thistlethwaite?" he repeated slowly. He sighed as he smiled fondly at the thought of his aunt though Miss Lilywhite's words were still working a considerable effect upon him. "Darling Aunt Euphemia is the world's greatest romantic, and nothing would please her more than to see me marry. Preferably someone poor and unsuitable—yet totally ravishing, like you—if only to spite her brother, since it was he who denied poor Aunt Euphemia the husband of her choice."

She looked tender when he said that, as if she were capable of caring, when just a moment before he'd been impressed by the flash of fire in Violet's eyes when she'd rebuked him for changing the subject; for talking of last night. She truly was beautiful, and she appealed to his senses on all levels.

"I think the easiest is to just go along with it."

"Just go along with it?" She looked as if he were mad. Her eyelashes fluttered and her lips pursed. Over her shoulder Max could see several other young women of similar age to Miss Lilywhite. They might have turned heads if they were not competing with the beauty in front of him. They certainly were not as adept at striking the right note. Miss Lilywhite seemed to know how to rise to any occasion with just the right degree of charm and admirable self composure. She was undeniably a talented actress.

"You're clearly not kept under lock and key in that house of ill repute or you'd not be here. And I'll pay you for your time, if that's what you're worried about?"

She blinked rapidly. "Lord Belvedere—"

"Call me Max, please. We're engaged."

"Alright. Max. But we're *not* engaged!"

"We are for the purposes of making my darling Aunt Euphemia happy, my dear Violet. I can call you that since we *are* engaged. She only has a few months to live, don't you know? You heard her cough, I suppose?"

"Yes, she coughed, but it didn't sound as bad as all that. Not like she was at death's door." Violet's mouth was pressed together into a tight line, and she was looking at him as if he'd taken leave of his senses when really, what he proposed was seeming more sensible by the minute.

"Well, I hope you're right and she's not going to die, Violet. I'm sure you hope that, too, since you said you liked her."

"Well, clearly I'd be delighted. But we can't carry on a ridiculous charade forever. And you'd have to set a wedding date. And there'd be guests and—"

"Yes, I know how weddings work. I've been involved in these preparations for months. I've been a marked man for years. Yes, for years it's been the assumption that Mabel and I would marry, even though no one consulted us until I was prodded into making it formal." It made him feel ill with relief at how close he'd come—yet survived. "And yes, we'll set a date."

"And it'll be a *second* wedding for you that doesn't go through? With all due respect, I don't think this is going to fill your Aunt Euphemia with the kind of joyful rapture you fondly imagine it will."

"Of course we'll go through with it. It'll be hush-hush. Just you and me and Aunt Euphemia and a couple of witnesses. A sham wedding. We'll pretend that we're off to the Continent, only I'll then embark for Africa and you can go back and do what you do, and everyone will be happy."

She looked disturbed by this when Max was suddenly feeling considerably pleased and clever. What a marvellous way to spend his last three weeks in England. He'd be making the greatest gesture possible towards Aunt Euphemia, who deserved so much for her maternal care of him all these years; he'd be adding to Miss Lilywhite's coffers in the process since she was, after all, a working girl who'd taken herself out of the marriage market by virtue of her profession so needed whatever coin she could to keep body and soul together.

"I fear it will not be as simple as you make it sound, Max."

"Nonsense!" he exclaimed, touching her cheek as he'd been wanting to do for some time now in order to remind himself of her softness. "We simply need to ensure our stories align, as you said." Yes, he was doing this for the happiness of his aunt, he reminded himself, as he added, "So, let's say we find somewhere quieter and more private to do just that."

CHAPTER 5

*V*iolet was conscious of the looks they received as she swept along the pavement, Max by her side. He was tall and handsome and she, although plainly dressed, had always received her fair share of admiration.

It had been a blessing and a bane her entire life. It's how she'd stumbled, then fallen into a profession that sucked dry all goodness from her soul.

It's why she was here, now, with a man who made her blood fizz in her veins like champagne as she contemplated the direction 'aligning their stories' might take.

"This is the house," she said after a few minutes' walk, indicating a tall, four-square residence set back from the street with a neat brick path leading to a black front door. Neat, respectable, and discreet.

And owned by a woman, equally so in each respect, who asked no questions as she handed them a key in exchange for Max's coins.

Violet didn't even blush. There was little point in false modesty when she was destined for hell anyway

"Do you come here often?" he asked as they mounted the stairs.

"I've never been here." She raised one eyebrow at his subtle quizzing. "My friend, Charity, uses it all the time though, as a place to meet her young man in private."

"My, my, he sounds accommodating."

"He was her first client." They'd reached their room at the end of the corridor, and Violet waited as Max inserted the key. She wanted to stroke the back of his head as he bent slightly. Instead, she added, "His grandfather had been horrified to learn his grandson was a virgin at twenty-three and so funded an educational evening at Madame Chambon's. Charity was also a virgin, so little help apparently. But they've been desperately in love for the past eighteen months. He pays most of his allowance to keep her exclusively. He's waiting until he comes into his inheritance when he turns twenty-five, so he can set her up properly. In the meantime, he brings her here whenever he can."

"A veritable lovers' nest." Indeed it was, Violet saw as Max threw open the bedroom door and they were met by the sight of a large, cushioned four-poster beneath a canopy of cream, gauzy bed hangings. The room was not large, but big enough to also accommodate a rose-velvet sofa by a merrily crackling fireplace.

"It has everything but the draughts board," Violet said on a soft laugh as she looked at the empty side table. But her insides were churning. She was achingly conscious of the man beside her, and she shivered in anticipation as she felt his fingertips slowly stroke her neck.

"I don't think I'm in the mood for draughts this evening." His voice was hoarse.

"Nor I." Violet heard the wanting in hers.

There was no need for words as she sank into his embrace. The cologne-imbued musky scent of his skin and the caress of his breath upon her cheek were all she needed to arch her neck and give him access to the buttons at her throat.

"You kiss very well, Lord Belvedere," she whispered as he worked the fastenings loose, and with commendable dexterity, slipped his hand into her bodice, then insinuated it beneath the layers of her underpinnings to cup her breast. Tingles of excitement charged up her spine as he fondled the nipple, at the same time as removing her jacket while Violet worked at her skirt fastenings.

Soon she was wearing nothing but her corset, chemise, and stockings, lying across the bed while he towered, shirtless, above her, his handsome face focused intently upon her as if she were the most prized morsel he'd hunted all day.

"How do you plan to explain our first meeting to your aunt, my Lord?" Violet asked, smiling up at him, her dark ringlets charmingly framed against the white pillows. "We've not much we can be truthful about."

"Damn the truth, my fair wench. I don't care what story you want to concoct. All I'm interested in is ravishing you this very moment."

She murmured a muffled agreement into his neck as he swooped upon her, his hand skimming the length of one thigh and rucking up her lawn petticoat at the same time. When it arrived at the juncture of her legs, she was wet with wanting, curling into him as she worked the buttons of his trousers.

"And I want you naked so I can see you," she whispered when she found her voice. "And *feel* you."

His touch was as sweet as it was achingly sensual. Violet had never been moved by intimacy with a man. Until now. She'd fancied herself in love before, but her initiation to lovemaking had been brief and disappointing. What followed had been even more disheartening and, after that, nothing but a series of charades.

This was real.

He pulled her against him when he was unashamedly naked, deftly unlacing her corset, whisking off her chemise, then burying his head between her breasts. Breathing her in deeply, he contoured her curves, his large, warm, gentle hands quickly finding the nub of her desire.

"So, *this* is where you like it?" he whispered, sliding his fingers through its moistness, causing Violet to shudder. "My sweet Violet, I am your slave."

"Just keep doing what you're doing," she returned, her body feeling boneless yet at the same time a seething mass of sensation.

She kissed the top of his head as he bent to his work. Burying her face in his light-brown curls, she surrendered herself completely, for the first time ever, to a man's tender ministrations.

For he was as tender as he was passionate, his hands smoothing her skin, fingers working their magic, bringing her to an ever-heightened awareness of what it was to truly feel the need of a man. And she pleasured herself through the mere touch of him, tracing his bones, his muscles, circling his nipples like they were delicate shells, skimming her hands over his flanks until she could grasp his rod, causing him to sink into the mattress on a groan.

"You are quite magnificent, sweet Violet, and I *want* you *now*."

"Then you shall have me," she vowed, wriggling over him, fusing her hips to his before he flipped her onto her back and loomed over her.

In the dim light, his eyes glowed and his mouth curved. "Are we ready for this?" he asked on a low rumble of a laugh as she shivered to feel the tip of his manhood seeking her entrance.

"As ready as you clearly are," she responded on a gurgle of happiness as she gave a little wriggle, inviting him in further.

Without another word, Max plunged into her in one smooth stroke, and Violet gasped her delight, and shuddered with excitement as she hooked her legs around his waist, wanting more than anything in that moment to *be* as one and to *feel* as one, as close and melded with another human being as was possible.

She'd been on the brink when he'd entered her, but his increasingly rapid thrusts sent her brain into a whirl of wicked pleasure, and her body into a morass of eternally damning ectasy so that her climax was beyond anything she could have imagined.

With a cry of delight, she shattered around him, her arms binding him to her as he collapsed with a groan of ecstasy, rolling over her so he didn't crush her.

"By gad, Violet, now *that* was the best tupping I've ever enjoyed!" His laugh was unrestrained as he squeezed her affectionately. "I feel like I'm going to die of pleasure." His breathing was rapid; his skin hot and slick with sweat. "Please, don't talk to me for a few minutes while I regain my strength. I think I'm going to want to do this all over again, very soon."

Obediently, Violet lay in silence, smiling at the ceiling, her body humming with contentment while the comforting warmth of Max's body seeped into her like a life-generating mantle of safety.

"We really should get down to business and discuss what we're going to tell your aunt," she said with real regret after a few minutes, sitting up and stroking his chest as she smiled down at him. "I'm going to have to leave you sooner than I'd like."

"Really?" He looked appalled. "You have to go?"

"In half an hour, I do. And it really is very important that we both decide how you're going to ask me to marry you." She bit her lips together to suppress the mirth that was ready to escape, even as he realised what she meant.

"My, my, but you're a funny girl, Violet," he chided, raising an eyebrow. "A clever one too, as I've already said—so I think I hardly need to remind you that this is all a charade."

"A *charade*? Did I not give satisfaction, my Lord?" she asked with mock indignation. "Did you not enjoy my willing wantonness and my clever moves as much as last time? After what you said just now?"

"Do stop, my dear. I enjoyed it far too much for a man aspiring to a measure of chivalry, and I'd be too aggrieved to think that you, in fact, were only pretending to please me and to be pleased."

"It was all genuine enough." She sighed, running her hands over his chest. "Unfortunately. For I could think of nothing nicer than to do this with you on a very regular basis. But I'm not the hopeless romantic your aunt is. Experience has made me pragmatic, and so I will simply appreciate the next three weeks until I must farewell you to Africa and hope you'll remember me when you return."

He sat up and stroked her hair, tidying a ringlet by smoothing it around his finger. "What a gem you are, Violet. All right then, how would I ask you to marry me?" He was softly stroking her breasts as he murmured this. Then gently spanning her waist with his hands as he moved her off the bed and onto the floor where they stood, naked, face to face.

"I think there should be an orchestra playing," he said, as he raised one hand to her shoulder, the other still round her waist. "A gentle waltz should be playing in the background and your—" He broke off, adding, "Yes; your head would be resting against my chest, just like that, as we circled the floor, the scent of summer drifting through the open French doors. And I'd look down at you and whisper, 'Violet, I don't think I can live without you. Will you marry me?' "

Violet raised her head to look at him. She knew her eyes were moist, and she didn't care. She raised her hand to touch his cheek. "I've known that for a long time, darling," she whispered. "I've just been waiting." She sighed, shaking herself back to reality as she managed a watery smile. "There, that should satisfy your aunt."

For a moment, he was silent. "Yes, it should." His tone was sober as he took her hand and led her to the sofa by the fire, dragging the counterpane from the bed to cover them both as they sank down onto the velvet.

He took both her hands in his. "How did you come by this way of life?" he asked.

Caught by surprise, Violet gave a short laugh. "We don't want to mix fact with fiction here, Max. Let's just concoct our fantasy for your aunt's sake. That way we'll not run the risk of being exposed."

He gave a half nod. "I suppose you're right."

"So, now that you know how you asked me to marry you, how did you *meet* me? When did you fall in love with me?"

He sent her a mischievous smile. "I'll confess to being as big a romantic as Aunt Euphemia. When did I meet you? When did I know I was in love with you? Why, like you, lovely Violet, it was love at first sight. Yes, I fell in love with you the moment I set eyes on you."

"And where did you set eyes on me?"

He squinted at her. "You're testing me, aren't you? You've already told Aunt Euphemia, and you told me too." He raised his eyes to the ceiling, thinking. "You worked in a shop. A haberdasher's. Yes! And I stepped over the threshold looking for gentleman's handkerchiefs and was served by you. The most stunning creature I'd ever laid eyes upon."

"Aren't you sweet, darling."

"I do like the way that rolls off your tongue."

"The way what rolls off my tongue?"

"The endearment. And a great many other things. Are you sure you don't have time for another—?"

"I wish! But no, Max." Violet rose, gripping the counterpane against her chest and taking a few steps away, turning to cast an incisive look at the evidence of his desire. "My Lord, but you are magnificently endowed. It has been a *pleasure!*"

With a shout of laughter, Max leapt up and snatched the counterpane from her grasp, whisked her into his arms and carried her to the bed.

"What can't we achieve together, and in five minutes?" he growled, dropping her onto the mattress and caging her body with his. "Do say yes, my darling."

"Yes, yes, and yes!" she cried, her heated body so ready for his frenzied kisses. "I think I'd say yes to *anything* you asked of me—but I think you also know that."

"All I know is that you're the most delightful morsel I've ever tasted," he responded, coming up from between her legs and kissing her roundly on the mouth. "Now, let round two begin! I honestly don't think I can get enough of you! Yet, alas, this will be our last time engaging in such sport if I've an ounce of chivalry in my bones."

CHAPTER 6

*J*n her cosy sitting room, Aunt Euphemia gazed fondly at Max who, with a great deal of throat clearing, said the words he knew she'd been wanting to hear.

He knew she wanted to hear them because she'd said only several nights earlier, "Darling Max, nothing could make me happier than for me to receive the news that you had in fact asked the girl of your heart to become your wife."

Clapping her hands together now, she rose and swept across the room to enfold him in her violet-scented embrace.

The cool of her cheek was a well-remembered comfort, but the violet scent sparked a new emotion to life. He must remember to buy Violet both flowers and scent to honour her name. She'd like that.

"Your cousin Emma will be overjoyed for she has just as soft a heart as I do." Then, more gravely, "Your grandfather will come around when he realises how much further a man can go with a good woman by his side. Regardless of her origins. And that's what a match of the heart will promote. Harmony which leads to success. A marriage should not be restricted by pecuniary considerations."

"Did you not agree that grandfather should be kept in the dark until the deed is done, Aunt?" Max patted her hand and led her back to her seat. Lowering himself into a wingback chair opposite, he said over steepled fingers, "Truly, I would beg you to keep this in the strictest confidence."

"Oh Max, you're going to elope? No, please don't say it?" Aunt Euphemia's face dropped. "Why, the poor young woman will suffer terribly from the shame of it. She'll miss all the joy of planning the most joyous occasion of her life. Believe me, I know this from my heart."

"I think my Violet is somewhat different to you, Aunt, but I will bear it in mind. The young lady is an orphan…" he had to think quickly about this "…and earns her living through her own means—"

Aunt Euphemia cut him off, clicking her tongue as she sympathised. "An orphan? How tragic! And she works in a haberdashery. What hard work that must be, but I would have done it rather than lived my life alone as a spinster. Still, I can provide what others cannot, and it would be a pleasure." The enthusiasm returned to her tone. "I want to take her shopping, Max. I'll buy her a wedding gown and her trousseau. If she's the girl who has stolen your heart, then she's as dear to me as my own daughter would have been."

Her lip trembled as she dabbed at her eyes with a handkerchief. She looked small and frail seated on the cream chintz sofa of the femininely decorated private sitting room in Lord Granville's townhouse that Max always thought so crowded during his grandfather's rare visits to the city.

Squaring her shoulders, a crafty light stole into her expression, and she clapped her hands. "Indeed, let's tell her this very minute! Come, Max. We'll go to her place of employ and surprise her!"

"Dear Aunt, she's…working. Or resting," Max added

beneath his breath. "We cannot disturb her now. I think she would be embarrassed."

"Then we shall go immediately to her place of abode so I might leave a note, myself. I want to know this young lady, Max. I don't have long; you remember. What do I care for proprieties?"

A little more than you might think if the truth were revealed, thought Max, who only said, unconvincingly, "We will send a note round, shall we?"

"We shall get into the carriage this moment, Max, and find her. She's not a slave to these people she works for, surely? No, I can't wait a moment longer."

Max, who thought this could only go badly, was astonished by the results of the hastily scrawled note he'd sent ahead with his manservant, Baines.

While he was delaying his aunt as best he could, he had thrust his note into Baines's hand and hissed that he must discreetly forward the letter to its recipient and Max would explain everything at the first opportunity.

But here was Miss Lilywhite smiling serenely at them from a table at the Lyons Teahouse, presenting herself as she no doubt had presented herself to his aunt, in a modest skirt and blouse which made her look every inch the smart shop girl Aunt Euphemia imagined her to be.

"Why, I told Max you'd come rushing to meet us at the first opportunity," his aunt said as if she could take all the credit. With a satisfied look at Max, then Violet, she said majestically, "The perfect pair. Handsome. Made for each other."

And then she proceeded to tell Violet her plans for the next two weeks, leading up to the secret wedding Max had proposed, embellishing it with all the details Max knew would occupy her with the greatest pleasure.

"What do *you* think of all this, Max darling?"

Max reacted to Violet's question with a guilty jolt. What he'd really been thinking was how deliciously desirable Violet looked in her neat black suit. A siren dressed up as a lady of demure disposition, and only he knew it. It made him feel supremely fortunate.

Instead, he murmured, "I was thinking how beautiful you looked," as he reached across the table for her hand.

Amused, he saw the colour creep into her cheeks as she bent her head.

Aunt Euphemia sighed. "Why, the pair of you are quite delightful. And to think, Max, that I had no idea marriage with Mabel was simply an act of duty."

Violet flashed him a wicked smile. "Max is the most dutiful man I've ever met, Miss Thistlethwaite. Honourable, dutiful, and quite the *handsomest* man of my acquaintance. Believe me, I see many in my line of work."

Max blinked as his aunt murmured, "I'm sure you do. I've heard gentlemen can be most exacting when they're after for something in particular."

"Very," agreed Violet. She smiled. "I've learnt to be patient." She sighed. "But Max was not difficult at all. That's why I fell in love with him."

The way they were both looking at him as if he were an Adonis in terms of moral virtue, as well as physical attributes, made him realise the need to put an end to it.

"Please, Violet, I think you're doing it a little too brown."

"Goodness no, Max! You're simply too modest." She reined in her amusement and pushed back her shoulders. "But what do you really think of all this, Max? Your aunt is proposing to expend a great deal of money on me. I have nothing to contribute other than my company on the myriad exploits she's just outlined. I'm beyond gratified, but I do think perhaps her generosity is beyond what is—"

"No, no, my dear, nothing would give me more pleasure!" Miss Thistlethwaite protested.

Gently, Max patted Violet's wrist. "No one will think any the worse of you for accepting what is given with the greatest of good hearts." The fondness in his smile was as much for his aunt as it was for Violet. "Now, I believe you two ladies have some shopping to do while I have some plans to make regarding our wedding tour. Venice, my love? What could be more romantic? Indulge Aunt Euphemia and you'll be indulging me. I think you'll find her enjoyment fully equal to yours throughout this venture."

EXCEPT THAT VIOLET WAS WISE ENOUGH TO KNOW HER enjoyment would be fast evaporating as the execution of their little charade for Miss Thistlethwaite's benefit reached its conclusion.

Still, she'd not lied when she'd told Max that a healthy pragmatism had helped her through life, though she did feel guilty as she waited for Miss Thistlethwaite at the entrance to what was supposedly London's most fashionable modiste.

Her guilt was only exacerbated by the genuine pleasure in her new benefactress's expression, as Miss Thistlethwaite extended an arm in welcome before gesturing Violet to accompany her up the stairs to the studio of 'a French woman of the greatest discernment.'

Violet couldn't help but draw an uncomfortable parallel. Madame Chambon considered herself such a personage, but the tall, elegant French modiste who briskly attended to Violet's measurements was a league apart from the gross creature who directed Violet's life.

Still, how wonderful it was to forget all that for a few moments as she held out her arms so that the guipure-lace sleeves might be fitted to the tight princess-line bodice in a manner that would do justice to 'Miss Lilywhite's perfect form,' while Miss Thistlethwaite offered an enthusiastic commentary from the Chippendale chair that had been arranged for her beneath an arched window.

"Of course, you must decide exactly how the gown shall look. Pay no mind to the fact I'm paying for it. Too vulgar to put that into words. However, when I was planning my own wedding gown after Richard offered so gallantly, I chose…"

It wasn't difficult to see how genuinely affected Miss Thistlethwaite was by the dismissal of her former suitor at the hands of her callous brother, and as Violet was uncomfortably mindful of the fact that her own preparations were no more than a farce, she was eager to allow Miss Thistlethwaite to channel her own thwarted dreams into Violet's wardrobe.

"Oh, my dear, but it is easy to see why Max loves you so." Miss Thistlethwaite dabbed her eyes with a scrap of lace before running her admiring gaze from the hem of Violet's swathed satin skirt to the veil of finest netting. "You are a vision. A vision in your daily attire, but what will he think when he sees you have become the fairy tale princess of his dreams?"

Violet felt it, too. The exhilaration of becoming, even more, an object of admiration and desire. She wanted Max to see her as a princess, a *lady*. Not what he knew her to be.

"Yet what are clothes when it's all in the heart?" Miss Thistlethwaite tapped her chest. "I'd have happily forgone all the trappings my brother considered necessary to a person of my standing."

From the French modiste to Lyon's teahouse on the second day of their furious pursuit of clothes, Miss Thistlethwaite showed as much eagerness as if she were the intended bride, prompting Violet to ask, "Is it true that your brother refused to sanction your marriage because he deemed your suitor unworthy, despite your feelings?"

Miss Thistlethwaite nodded. "My Richard went to see him, cap in hand. I was sure Septimus would relent, eventually. It wasn't as if there were any other prospective husbands lined up. I was twenty-five. Decidedly on the shelf and possessed of neither wit nor good looks." Her smile was wry. "It's hard to imagine my handsome Max is my own flesh and blood. Such a magnificent creature. Oh, but you and he will be so happy together!" She clasped her hands together. "Tell me, how *did* he propose?"

Violet's lighthearted mood had been swept away by the thought that the kindly woman opposite her had spent the past three decades lonely and disregarded. Now the weight of duplicity was added to her burden.

"Max hasn't told you?" she asked cautiously.

Miss Thistlethwaite shook her head. "He hasn't, no, though it's clear enough how happy he is." Again, her eyes filled with moisture. "What a pleasure it is to me to see true love shining from both of you like a beacon of hope. It's my compensation," she added softly. Then, more eagerly, "But do tell me, Violet."

Violet lowered her eyes to her hands that were fidgeting in her lap. Lying didn't sit well with her, but she supposed it was in a good cause. She smiled, remembering. Yes, remembering the way Max had drawn her from the bed and into his arms, tenderly waltzing her, naked, about the room, describing the scene as he'd offered her his pretend marriage proposal.

She could see it in her mind's eye as if it had really happened. Except that she was...

"...wearing a lilac gown I'd made myself, Miss Thistlethwaite, and the orchestra was playing Brahms." She smiled, closing her eyes, shivering as if she really could feel the soft pressure of Max's hands upon her waist and shoulder. "Max had taken me to this marvellous place, and I thought myself the luckiest young woman in the entire world. Even luckier when he asked me to marry him, for I knew I…didn't deserve him."

"My goodness, enough of such talk. You, Violet, are the most deserving young woman I've met. You work hard; you never complain, and…you love Max. That is all that is important in my mind. That my darling Max enjoy a union where love blooms mutually." She patted Violet's hand for Violet knew her expression had closed. *Deserving* was not a description that sat comfortably with her, either.

"Max lost his mother *so* young. He's been looking for love ever since and, like Septimus, I suppose, I thought Mabel was his perfect match. They'd known one another since they'd been children, and they seemed to get along like a house on fire. They were always so comfortable in one another's company. But that's not romantic love. I should have realised that. But tell me, exactly how long have you known one another?" Miss Thistlethwaite looked like an eager dormouse with her bright eyes seeking from Violet crumbs of happiness she might feast upon in her mind when she returned to her, no doubt, lonely apartments in her brother's townhouse.

"A little over a year. He first took me to see a play," Violet said slowly, thinking about an interest the two of them shared. "The play was set in exotic lands and, as you know, Max loves adventure—"

"Oh, he does indeed. Mabel didn't, which is why it's not so surprising she left him. That takes spirit, in my mind. But we won't talk about that. It's all worked out for the best. You now, Violet, are a woman with an adventurous spirit. One can see it in your eyes. So, what was this play about? Was it set in Africa or India, two of the very places Max is so eager to see?"

"In India. It was set in India, which is where I was born. He was interested to hear that and it…it brought us closer together because I could describe it to him. The colours, the vibrancy." Violet looked through the window and remembered how much she'd loved India.

But Miss Thistlethwaite was prodding her for more information. What had she been telling the old lady? She'd forgotten. The life she'd led in India was so different from the one to which she'd been consigned in England. Harder, but free in a way she wasn't, here. It had been a life of discovery and exploration. The curiosities her father had discovered. The reverence with which he'd shown Violet and her sister. Exquisite butterflies of cobalt blue with yellow markings. Emily had cried when she'd accidentally crushed one in her chubby little fist. Violet had said its spirit had been released in a new world and not to despair.

Emily had asked if *her* spirit would do the same one day. Violet wondered if it had.

"My dear, you are crying! But of course, a proposal is a time for tears, is it not? I remember how I cried, too." Miss Thistlethwaite's tone changed. "But you are *sad*? Oh, my dear, I'm so sorry. I didn't mean to pry. You were saying you were born in India. You told Max about it. Tell me, do you miss it?" Miss Thistlethwaite was speaking fast now, trying to deflect Violet but her words only made it worse.

"I miss it terribly."

"Then Max will take you back there. He wants to see India, and he'd do anything in his power to make you happy. I could see it in his eyes the way he looked at you. You can see your family again. They are there, now, are they not? That is why you're so sad. You miss them."

Violet shook her head, and the tears that she'd managed to delicately contain were suddenly unleashed in a torrent.

"They're not there. Or rather, they are buried there."

"Oh, my poor girl." Miss Thistlethwaite put her hands to her cheeks. "Both of them?"

Violet nodded. "Yes, both of them. They were murdered in Cawnpore."

Max fiddled with his cufflink as he stood in the theatre foyer and waited for Violet to appear. Aunt Euphemia had bought tickets for them all to attend a performance of *As You Like It* at Drury Lane. She would be bringing Violet in her own carriage as Violet had insisted she'd get herself to Miss Thistlethwaite's townhouse—or rather, her brother's—due to her 'working commitments'.

Of course, Aunt Euphemia had understood Violet's meaning in quite a different way. However, to Max, standing alone for the moment as he toyed with the gold monogrammed studs at his wrists, the idea caused him more angst than it ought.

Violet was a charming creature he'd essentially bought for her services for three weeks. The fact she was proving so bewitching in every way to him, and apparently so delightful to his aunt, should be neither here nor there. A very generous sum had been agreed upon for the whole transaction. And that didn't even include his aunt's largesse in terms of clothes and meals in fine restaurants and teahouses.

The moment Max and Violet had said their fictional vows

and gone their separate ways, Violet would receive the second and final part of the agreed-upon sum in a nominated bank account which Max had set up.

He couldn't help but admire Violet's surprisingly specific stipulations. Of course, she'd never been in receipt of funds in this manner before; however, she'd been quite specific in terms of how she was to be paid—into a bank account that Max had set up in her name of which she, alone, was the signatory. Very novel.

However, this was the only way she'd have access to a line of credit that Madame Chambon could not touch, much less be aware of.

Violet Lilywhite was a surprising creature in so many ways. And the more Max learnt of her beyond the bedroom, the more there was to admire.

Which was extremely discomforting when he actually had time to reflect upon her as a person beyond the narrow scope to which he'd initially relegated her.

Yes, it was extremely discomforting that an image of her sparkling blue eyes kept intruding into his consciousness whenever he had a moment's reflection. Or that he'd find himself wanting to seek her out for her opinion.

Or run his hands over her satin-smooth skin and lose himself in her embrace.

Which, of course, he couldn't even do now, despite wanting to very much, as she swept into the foyer at his great-aunt's side; tall, slender, majestic, those exquisite eyes lighting up at the sight of him. She was altogether the most magnificent woman he'd ever encountered.

But he had to remind himself very forcefully; he was not looking for a wife.

And if he were, she was the most unsuitable wife he could have chosen. Society would vilify them all if he made any kind of proposal that transgressed the boundaries carved out in stone. Boundaries beyond which not even the boldest cavalier thumbing his nose at convention would consider stepping beyond.

Now she was placing her hand upon his arm, an action that instantly aroused every nerve end.

That's why he must remember she was not wife material. She was a woman whose calling was to create this very sensation in men.

All men. It was her job.

Still, he'd be lying if he didn't admit he'd rather be here this evening with her than in any other company.

"Doesn't your fiancée look beautiful?" Aunt Euphemia demanded, as if he were lacking in gallantry.

His aunt looked better than he'd seen her look in a very long time. There was a healthy glow to her skin, and her voice was strong and eager.

"Words failed me for a moment, Aunt Euphemia." He smiled at Violet after a brief look of acknowledgment at the old lady, then lowered his voice, his intimate tone both as much for his aunt's benefit as the obvious recipient, "How lucky I am that I'll be able to call you my wife in a couple of weeks."

"Yes, you are, Max. Lucky, indeed." His aunt encompassed them both in a look of great fondness. "Violet and I spent a very pleasant afternoon yesterday having tea after her final fitting for her wedding gown." She sighed. "Only ten days until your wedding. Truly, I will miss her when you are gone."

Clearly, a look of dismay must have shown itself in Max's face, which Violet misinterpreted for playacting when, in fact, he was digesting the fact that after ten days, he would never see her again.

"Your aunt has asked me all about our wedding tour, darling. To the Continent." Violet's smile was meaningful. "I know only of plans for Venice but apparently there's a great deal more to look forward. Naturally, those are details only you are privy to."

"Yes, of course." He looked at Aunt Euphemia. "Shrouded in mystery, I'm afraid, Aunt. I'm making all manner of clandestine plans so that Violet is completely caught by surprise and delight. You know she's never been out of England?"

"But...I thought Violet said she'd been born in India." Aunt Euphemia's brow creased. She looked, in fact, quite distressed as she turned to Violet. "I thought you said that's where your parents are buried."

Violet nodded as she put her hand on his aunt's. "I'm sorry if I upset you with my story yesterday, Miss Thistlethwaite. Actually, I haven't told Max everything I should have about my life. I like to pretend it began, and will finish, here in England. Those years in India were colourful but, ultimately, painful." She smiled at them both and turned the subject. "Now, I believe the play is about to begin."

When Max finally had her to himself, as they chatted in the dim window embrasure during the interval while his aunt spoke to several acquaintances whom Max had made sure were far enough away they'd not be introduced to him, he said, "You were very adept in the way you deflected my aunt who was clearly troubled by the discrepancy in our stories. Or rather, our knowledge. Just shows how much I need a clever wife like you to guide me." He grinned at her and couldn't help but reach out to touch the bare skin at her wrists. It was, sadly, all that he could be satisfied with at this juncture. "I must say, you're working out very well in this role. You've been very sporting. I hope you're having fun." He scanned her face. "It's not too much pressure on you to keep up such a deception?" He didn't expect a rebuttal. Violet had been nothing but a pleasure during the ten days they'd been involved in their charade. If anyone had been under pressure, it had been Max. He'd seen her every day in his aunt's company but, alone, only at Madame Chambon's the night he'd met her, and that one gloriously abandoned afternoon at the discreet house of assignation to which she'd taken him.

Yet even while his body had throbbed for her, something at the back of his mind had warned him that to get any closer could be disastrous. Perhaps it was his gentle aunt's inevitable horror that he'd been using the girl in such a way. Yes, he was paying her well, but to do a specific job that did not entail buying her body. That went against the grain when it came to any notion he held of being an honourable man. If no money had changed hands, Max would have availed himself of her willing charms with as much enthusiasm as the next unscrupulous fellow.

And, besides all that, he realised he was becoming dangerously addicted to her company.

"All part of my job," she said smoothly. "I aim to give satisfaction." Her lovely eyes sparkled, and her mouth quirked before she added with an edge of seriousness "Though if I am guilty of any transgression, unwittingly though it would be, you must tell me. Your aunt is a dear soul, and I would hate to think that what started as such a kindly motivated deception might cause her pain."

"She is very fond of you so yes, another slip-up like the one a little earlier could cause her a great deal of pain, not to mention shame and embarrassment. I should hate that. However, it's been a pleasure to see how much she's enjoying herself." He couldn't help smiling at the simple pleasure of reflecting upon how much his aunt was throwing herself into turning Violet into the bride she'd never been. He cleared his throat. "She told me she thinks of you as the daughter she never had." He had mixed feelings about this. Max loved his aunt dearly, and he only hoped that when he and Violet supposedly left the country on their protracted wedding tour, Aunt Euphemia would not be too bereft. Still, he was sure that both she, and he, would settle back quickly into the old routine. Violet would only have been a part of their lives for a few short weeks and Max was off to Africa in less than three weeks.

"My dear Violet, the only pain you've caused her was by possibly overstretching the mark with your little story about your parents. Murdered?" His mouth quirked. "My aunt does love a dramatic story, but that was perhaps doing it a bit too brown."

He'd glanced a moment over her shoulder at a cluster of theatre patrons near the door, but when he looked back at her, he saw her face had drained of colour, and for one ghastly moment he thought he was the cause by suggesting she'd fabricated the story. Good God, was it *true*?

Then her hand was clutching her heart and she was clearly trying to keep her equilibrium as she whispered, "Lord Bainbridge is on the other side of the room, and he's seen me."

Max turned, an unaccountable spurt of pure jealousy curdling his earlier pleasure. Foolish, really, when there was no deception between Violet and himself or any of the men in her life, including Lord Bainbridge.

"Should I be concerned?" he asked drily, and was ashamed by the look she gave him. She'd have no idea how carefully he'd effected his tone of unconcern.

"Do you mean have I offered him exclusivity?" she asked, intimating that keeping company with Max would give Bainbridge grounds for calling him out. "No, I have not." She sighed and sent Max a rueful look. "But I have been hoping he'd ask for it. Still." She brightened. "Perhaps you will be more useful to me than I'd imagined. A little jealousy on his part might be the impetus he needs." Under her breath, she added, "Just make sure your aunt doesn't arrive at the wrong time. Ah, good evening Lord Bainbridge." She turned. "I trust you are acquainted with Lord Belvedere?"

Max was impressed. Her poise was admirable as was her skill in managing a conversation that might have fired discontent in either gentleman's breast. By the end of a few minutes Lord Bainbridge was backing away, clearly reluctant to relinquish the hand he'd bent over to kiss in farewell.

"You have him just where you want him, my beautiful vixen," Max complimented her reluctantly. "I think you need have no fear that your future is not secure beyond..." he hesitated, not liking to put into words the fact that Violet's tenure in his own life would be ending so soon. A frisson of something hard to identify—regret, concern—made him want to launch into a volley of questions he'd not thought to ask before when their association was in the nature of business only.

It was hard to remember that sometimes.

"I don't take anything for granted, Lord Belvedere." He'd expected her tone to be light, but she was staring after Lord Bainbridge with a strange look in her eye.

And once again Max found he desired greatly to know what she was thinking.

But now was not the place to ask. And, really, it was not *his* place to ask.

CHAPTER 8

It was a relief to be back with Miss Thistlethwaite, who reminded Violet of her own kindly grandmother. Her mother's mother, now deceased, *not* her father's.

She shivered, and Max, solicitously asking if she were cold, rested his hand protectively over the small of her back creating the most inconvenient tendrils of desire.

"No, but I think your aunt may be," she said more tartly than she'd intended as she moved away and bent over Miss Thistlethwaite, who was seated on a banquette in the corner.

"You look suddenly very tired, Miss Thistlethwaite. Would you like to leave?" she asked. The festivities had been a novelty, but now Violet was as exhausted as Miss Thistlethwaite looked with the need to act a part she increasingly had no desire to play.

It had been a joy to again inhabit a venue where she rubbed shoulders with London's upper echelons, but painful too. She felt no concern at being recognised. That was not the cause of her growing despondency. In fact, she'd have been pleased to have met someone of her old acquaintance and for word to have filtered back home. Let her shame attach to *them*. To those who'd sent her on this awful journey.

But being in Max's company was always a pleasure—as well as a reminder that she'd have him for so short a time. Regardless of the position in society she'd once held, the fact was that Violet was a creature beyond redemption. Fallen women did not become the wives of men like Max, even if Max had been prepared to alter his plans and marry her instead of seeking adventure across the seas.

Miss Thistlethwaite coughed delicately, began to speak, and then found she couldn't stop coughing. "I don't want to be a killjoy," she finally managed. She looked grey and desperately fatigued, and Violet was worried.

The old lady smiled. "It's rare for the two of you to have an opportunity to be together, and I know, Violet, that you must return to your grandmother as soon as you've left this place."

It was a useful lie that Violet had perpetuated during the past few days, but now she shook her head. "You've been so kind to chaperone me this evening, but I assure it'll be no hardship to take you home. Max and I have the rest of our lives to spend together and right now, I feel more than ready for my bed."

She glanced about the crowded foyer of the theatre. The beautiful clothes and sparkle of jewels stirred her senses. The scent that perfumed the air seemed rarefied and reminiscent of her old life. As her gaze rested on the ermine-lined bodice of a chic Worth gown—yes, she was sure it was by the designer, Worth—she felt like a creature from another planet. Not that she didn't belong, but that she'd been in a different galaxy a very long time before being transported home.

Yet finding a home had been her goal since she'd been banished from her grandmother's; in fact, since she and

Emily had swapped India's warmth and colour for the grey dreariness of England following her parents' brutal deaths.

When Emily had been alive, Violet had been fuelled by the urgency to create one for a young and innocent sister who needed one even more than Violet. Since Emily's death, the urgency had subsided. Nevertheless, Violet *would* have a place to call home one day. Perhaps a small cottage in a quiet seaside town. As long as she had security, what did it matter that the funds to purchase it derived from a line of work that depended on her beauty and her acting skills.

Glancing from Miss Thistlethwaite to Max, she caught him looking down at her with an odd expression on his face. The moment they locked glances, his frown of slight puzzlement transformed into pleasure.

And that familiar feeling of want and need and desire that had been her undoing all those years ago washed through her body like a king tide.

Only this time it was so much stronger and more dangerous than before.

She straightened, patting Miss Thistlethwaite on the shoulder, conscious of the fragile, birdlike bones beneath her hands.

She'd grown fond of Miss Thistlethwaite, but the old lady was dying. Everything she loved died. She must remember that.

Just as well that Max had insisted upon playing the gentleman since their last lustful encounter.

Love could not be depended upon, and sentiment made her susceptible to unwise decisions. "Come, Max," she said. "It's time to take your aunt home."

~

"I WAS MASTERFUL, WAS I NOT?"

Violet smiled at Max as he rested his head against the carriage window. He was looking at her, again with that expression of curiosity and interest. And undisguised admiration. He often praised her. Her beauty and her wit. It made her forget herself sometimes and feel she was on his level. That she was the kind of woman she'd once been.

"You're always masterful, Max."

It was true. Kind and masterful. A potent combination though she wouldn't tell him that. Just as she wouldn't tell him a great many other things she'd have liked. Baring her heart had never been a good idea. She'd learnt that from experience.

"However, being masterful in this instance won't get you what you want, for all that your aunt was very acquiescent to your persuasion that you see her home first, and now we're alone in your carriage. As I said earlier, I'm very tired."

"You said you were more than ready for your bed. I distinctly heard you say it." He grinned at her, confident he'd win her over.

She was equally confident he wouldn't. She'd been disappointed when he'd passed up earlier opportunities to sleep with her, but now she understood that his motivation came from the same sources as hers right now—he wanted to protect himself. The chemistry of their last, unforgettable physical encounter had been dangerously unsettling.

"It's too late to get a room at that discreet establishment I took you to, and you won't come to Madame Chambon's. You've already made it quite clear you'll never step over the threshold of an establishment of that nature, and I applaud your high morality"

He cut her off. "No, not Madame Chambon's. I shall never darken the doorstep of a place like that again." The furrow between his eyes deepened. "When I marry, I shall have no one else. My wife deserves a man of moral conviction."

"And she'll be a lucky woman. But please stop doing that, Max. You shan't win me over with your gentle back stroking or your winning looks. I'm tired."

"Yes, you look quite done in, if you don't mind me saying it." He was undeterred, clearly in top form after an evening which had only confirmed how much freedom he had as a gentleman of high standing; the way he'd sauntered with such confidence through the throngs at a society event where he was made welcome by all. His future was assured.

"Max, don't! I told you!" Immediately she'd snapped out the words she was contrite. "I beg your pardon. I had no right"

"No, I had no right." He wasn't smiling now. He drew back a little but, as the carriage rounded the corner to Albemarle Street, he leaned forward and tentatively extended his hand though he didn't touch her. "Why Violet, that's surely not a tear? Have I offended you *so* much?"

"I don't know why I should be crying, and please don't say that it's beyond you why a woman like me should cry over such a matter."

"Good God, so that is the reason you're crying. Because I pushed myself on you?"

"You hardly did that, Max." Violet closed her eyes as she leant her head against the cushioned squabs of the carriage interior. "Pay me no mind. I'm being very foolish. Thank you for a lovely evening." With an effort, she stirred but as she shifted towards the door, the horses sprang into motion and she was pushed back against the seat again and Max's voice was intruding, loud but anxious, "Don't look so frightened. I'm not kidnapping you, but I can't possibly see you leave when you're clearly upset. We can drive about while you tell me exactly what's troubling you. Is it me? Have you lost your heart for this charade? Are there better fish to fry? Men who'll pay you more money?"

"How dare you!?"

He nodded. "Good, I was hoping to see your fiery spirit return by such a caddish remark." He crossed his arms and regarded her steadily. "So, out with it. Why are you upset?"

She shrugged and shook her head, not knowing how she could even explain it to herself.

"Have I done something wrong?"

"No, you've behaved with honesty and transparency. I'm not used to that. Perhaps I was crying because I don't know when I'll next meet a man who offers me something with no hidden caveats, or broken promises."

"Ah." Despite the clip-clop of the horses' hooves and the creak of harness, it was suddenly very quiet inside the carriage. "And you don't expect anything beyond that?"

"Of course I don't! Surely you don't imagine that I do." She was upset he might attribute hidden designs to her.

"I don't. Most women in your position would, I imagine."

She shrugged. "It's so easy to imagine that would be the case."

"What do you mean?"

"You think we're all the same. That prostitutes are all motivated by the same thing."

Max blinked. "I haven't thought much about it at all, I have to be honest." He looked concerned. "That paints me in a very entitled light, doesn't it?"

"You are entitled. That's all right. I understand. We are all who we are because we're shaped by our circumstances. I don't expect enlightenment and compassion from the men who pay me."

"I wish you wouldn't say things like that. You could have found a better way of phrasing it without demeaning your-self. Besides, it makes you sound far too intelligent for the work you do. If you want to know the truth, the only time I ever think of you as a—"

"Prostitute."

He sighed and repeated the word grudgingly, adding, "Is when you say it yourself. So, tell me, why *did* you choose this path?"

She burst out laughing. "No woman chooses this path. It chooses them! Now, the carriage has gone around the block twice; we've had a lovely conversation; you've told me all you need to in order to satisfy myself as to the kind of man you are, and you are in no doubt as to the kind of woman I am. All pretences have been laid to rest and now I must claim mine."

"I'm not delivering you to Madame Chambon's just yet. I'm worried about you, Violet." He rapped on the roof and gave the coachman directions for his own home. "Now, before you object," he said, holding up his hand for silence, "let me assure you that I am paying you for your time, not the services you'll feel duty bound to render me." His determined expression was softened by a smile. "Yes, we have a contract, but that contract was quite specific in terms of you upholding a well-motivated charade that'll keep my aunt happy." He paused. "Not me. Last time I lapsed, but I'll not do it again. For fear of repeating myself, I am not in the habit of paying women for sex. I can find my own willing dalliances for free, thank you very much."

Violet managed a watery smile. "Much too noble, aren't you, Lord Belvedere? So now you propose to take me somewhere to talk to me because you're concerned that I'm unhappy." She paused and raised an eyebrow. "Yet you have no intention of doing anything else, even though you're paying for my time because that was not in the contract."

He nodded. "Exactly. You're my greatest challenge all of a sudden, lovely Violet. See, we're at my townhouse. The servants are asleep, including the butler and manservant. There is no danger of anyone's reputation—including my own—being compromised provided you stay quiet."

"Stay quiet?" She managed a sceptical laugh. "Despite the onslaught of delights with which you'll no doubt shower me?"

"I told you. That's not my intention at all. We shall repair to my sitting room for a glass of champagne while we play draughts—at which I'll allow you to win this time. And we'll chat. Isn't that what you women love to do?"

She deliberately narrowed her gaze, and he raised his hands in the air in a gesture of supplication. "Yes, I'm humouring you, but if you must know, it's only to prove to myself that I can behave like a gentleman of honour under any situation."

"I hardly think there's any reason to feel embarrassed by your lapse last time." Violet studied her fingernails. "I enjoyed it more than I usually do." There, that should underscore the way it was between them even though it cheapened what had been, to her, a surprisingly rare and poignant intimacy.

Instead of meeting this with bluff good humour as she'd expected, he considered her a moment. Something indefinable flashed across his expression. If she didn't know better, she might have identified it as hurt.

But then his smile was back, and his tone was brisk, and he was holding out his hand to help her from the carriage. "Here we are. Half an hour and then I'll send you home. This is just to humour me, as you correctly said. Gentlemen don't like to think they can't live up to the expectations they've set themselves."

"Of course they don't." Violet didn't trouble to hide the cynicism in her tone. This was about him, not her. She'd be a fool to imagine that last time had been any different.

~

IN THE QUIET OF HIS PRIVATE APARTMENT ON THE FIRST FLOOR, she smiled at the draughts board already in place on the table.

"Premeditated, I see."

"Not at all. I often play draughts with myself." He positioned himself opposite her and indicated the board. "Black or white?"

"I daresay since you are used to being both, I won't be depriving you of a favourite if I choose white."

"In deference to your name, of course." He turned the board so her triangle of white pieces was positioned in front of her. "My grandfather was always white, too." He sent her a wicked grin. "So, it's little different from what I'm used to. I'm just playing a more attractive opponent. Now, your glass, Madam." He handed her a glass of fizzing liquid which Violet raised in salute.

Even before her first sip she was feeling surprisingly relaxed. Foolish girl.

His eyes sparkled at her over the top of the glass. "To what shall we toast?"

"That we are good enough at our little deception to bring tears of happiness to your aunt's eyes."

"That's rather sweet. I like that." He raised his glass. "To my dear aunt who, I must add, likes you very much, Violet. As do I."

"I know you do." Violet sent him a look that was half suggestive, half genuine. She couldn't decide how she felt. "Just not enough."

"Now, don't spoil it. I thought you were cleverer than that. We get along famously, and I shall look back at these few weeks with great fondness."

"When you're having your grand adventures shooting lions and evading headhunters in the African jungle."

He grinned. "Precisely. I can't wait to go, to be honest." Toying with one of the black pieces, he sighed. "Grandfather is dreadfully down on me for not persuading Mabel back to the negotiating table, but we're both determined not to be goaded into this thing, for all that it makes good financial sense."

"You make marriage sound dreadfully unromantic."

"Well, it isn't very romantic. Not for people like me." He topped up their glasses. "I have to marry a girl who fits my grandfather's criteria since I'm to inherit everything he has spent his lifetime safeguarding and building up. Do you know how hard it is to find a lifetime companion who won't drive one mad and who has the approval of the family?"

"So that's why you're running away to Africa?"

"Precisely." He nodded. "Self-preservation and to buy myself a few years. What choice do I have but to escape my family following this debacle with Mabel?" He finished his champagne and put down his glass. "I presume that's why you're throwing your youth and beauty into Lord Bainbridge's hands now that he's finally made you the offer you've been hoping for. He's hardly what I'd consider a particularly fine specimen of manhood."

"Jealous?" Violet teased.

Something flitted across his face again and then was gone. "Your turn," he said, bending over the board and studying the placement. "I still think you could do better than Lord Bainbridge."

"Beggars can't be choosers."

"And why are you a beggar, lovely Violet?" His eyes were bright with curiosity—or from the alcohol.

"You wouldn't believe me if I told you."

"No, I probably wouldn't." He shrugged. "You clearly have

an active imagination, though. I think Aunt Euphemia was suitably distressed to hear your parents had been…what did you tell her? Murdered."

Violet didn't say anything. What was there to say?

"Your turn to play, Violet." He waved his hand over the board, then hesitated as he was in the act of leaning back into the cushions. "I say, you're not offended, are you?" He cleared his throat. "I understand it's necessary for—"

She cut him off. "For girls like me to play fast and loose with the truth? There, Lord Belvedere, I just all but decimated you. Careless. You lost three."

He didn't look at the board. "Violet?" Then again, "Violet? Tell me what's wrong. You were sad in the carriage, and I brought you here to jolly your spirits. I thought I was doing a mighty fine job until just now. I'm sorry if I offended you by making light of what you choose to tell my aunt to elicit her sympathy. Bravo to you, I say. Aunt Euphemia loves a good tragic story"

"For God's sake will you stop harping on my storytelling!" Violet threw up her hands. "How many times can a girl take being called a liar and still smile about it? My parents were murdered. Are you satisfied? Yes, I told your aunt, but I spared her the details, and if you value our friendship as you say you do, goodness knows but talk like this is a strange way to go about cultivating it."

The temper had crept up upon her before she'd even been aware of it lurking in the shadows. Violet hadn't displayed temper since she'd been a child, so it took her by surprise. Unless this onslaught of emotion was something else altogether.

Surely it must be.

For why were the tears coursing down her cheeks as if she had no control of them?

Which she didn't.

Angrily, she brushed them away as she bent over the board, trying to focus.

But she couldn't. And then Max was by her side, holding her in his arms as so many suppressed memories found their outlet in her sobs.

She buried her face in his chest and breathed him in. Lemon verbena, sweat, horses. It was a good, honest smell that brought back the past even more strongly. "My dear girl, I had no idea. Truly, I am so sorry."

She could barely take in what he was saying. The sobbing wouldn't stop but he let her cry in silence, holding her and stroking her hair.

When finally she was exhausted from the emotion she leaned back, sighing deeply. "I should go." She made a move to rise but he wouldn't release her.

"Not until you've told me."

She shrugged. "My parents are dead. So are yours. It's all the same, in the end. The nature of their deaths is immaterial when you look at it like that. Grandmother ought to know," she added in a whisper, bitterness flooding her at the memory.

"My parents weren't murdered." He was serious now. "That's not something most of us have to live with. How did they die, Violet? Don't think I won't believe you," he added quickly.

"Their throats were cut. We were in Cawnpore—"

"Dear God!" The spasm of his shock reverberated through him as he held her. "I'm so sorry. And you really were living there? Forgive me, Violet. I thought"

"That everything I said about my past was a lie?"

"I supposed I was thrusting you into *my* lie. I just expected to get more of the same back." He touched her cheek. "I haven't really taken the trouble to listen to you properly. I've only…"

After a moment he asked, "Tell me all you want to but nothing you don't. I'll not pry, but I do want to help."

She chewed on her lip, the comfort of his arms around her transporting her back years to when she'd felt cherished. Safe.

"Please, Violet?"

She shivered. Could she bear to? Should she rake up the past? She'd never put any of this into words.

A tremor ran through her and his arms tightened around her. She rested her head on his chest and began to speak.

"My family lived in Cawnpore. My parents. Me. My sister." The thought of her sister made her smile. What he was asking her to remember didn't. "My father had a lucrative trading business and we lived well. A beautiful house, servants. I wanted for nothing." She'd been a privileged child, waited upon hand and foot. There'd been beautiful clothes and the lively tea parties her mother had enjoyed hosting.

It all seemed so long ago.

Closing her eyes and saying the words as Max stroked her face, felt like a dream. Before she'd even conjured the images, she remembered the smell. The damp earth smell that drifted through the half open window. The smell of the oil lamp on her father's desk.

The rank smell of evil, unwashed bodies as men who had no right to be there stole into the house.

"My parents had returned from dinner with the Governor. I heard them dismissing the servants, downstairs, after they returned. And then I must have fallen asleep for I was awoken by a strange commotion. A muffled cry, I realised afterwards when I hurried downstairs and discovered two bandits had entered the house. They were looking for valuables, I suppose, but my mother must have got in their way. My father, who'd been in his study, came into the drawing room at the same moment I did. When he saw they held a knife to Mother's throat, he had nothing with which to defend her. Or my sister or me. I've never seen a man look so helpless. We were all helpless. But Mother was like a lioness. She had a temper." Violet smiled. "You should have heard the insults she hurled. No, she didn't whimper in fright. But then my sister appeared. She'd been woken, too. She was only six and she didn't understand." Violet shrugged. "When one of the bandits came towards Emily, it was too much. Emily began to scream and Mother began to claw at her captor's eyes. That's when he sliced her throat. In the fight that ensued, I don't know what happened. It was all over so quickly. The bandits left. They took a few valuables. Only what they could snatch as they ran. And they left our parents dead at our feet."

Max's breathing was soft against the crackle of the fire. A ghostly silence enveloped them as he held her close and stroked her cheek. "My poor Violet. What happened to you, then?"

"As my mother's parents had died some years before, we went to live with my father's mother. She'd never approved of Mother, so her reception was not particularly rapturous."

Violet shuddered at the memory; at the flint in her grandmother's eye as if she blamed Violet and Emily for being alive when her son was not.

"How long ago was this?"

"Five, nearly six years ago. I was fifteen."

"Was your grandmother kind to you?"

"She fed and clothed us. She paid for decent clothes, fashionable enough not to invite censure upon her for being a poor guardian."

"But…you ran away? That's why you do what you do? Or is she dead? Did she leave you nothing?"

Clearly, it was a leap too far for him. And, of course

Violet couldn't expect him to know without being told. She'd come this far; she couldn't retreat.

But this was the part she didn't think she could put into words. Her parents' deaths had been beyond her control.

This had everything to do with her own youthful lack of control. She didn't know if she were ready to admit to her own failings and deficiencies to such an extent.

"I hesitate to tell you yet I daresay you can't think worse of me than you do." She sighed, speaking over his predictable protest. "When I was eighteen, we had guests. We lived in a large house in the village of Ruislip and two distant relatives came to stay. The gentleman was charming. At least, he was charmed by me, and I, who'd had no experience of the ways of men who want something from a woman was naïve enough to believe he found me attractive. I believed I was in love with him and that he'd take me away from my hateful grandmother. I dreamt of a life where I could be free. I imagined how we would take Emily with us and live our lives for one another. Without always feeling grandmother's dripping disdain for the daughters of the woman who'd lured her son away and been responsible for his death."

"But he didn't ask you to marry him?"

"He was in no position to though I didn't know it at the time."

She felt the tension in Max's grip. "He was married." He didn't have to make it a question.

"And I was despoiled. As it turned out, his wife was a dear friend of my grandmother's, and she painted me the seductress, though truth be told I'd never even smiled at a man before I met Ralph. Well, grandmother seized the opportunity to send me away to earn my own living."

"She cast you out? With nothing? Her own granddaughter had to fend for herself on the streets?"

"She paid me a small allowance which supplemented my

earnings from a position in a drapery. A respectable enough job, I suppose, as long as she didn't have to be troubled by me anymore. But it was the least she could do. As you pointed out, I was her granddaughter."

He didn't ask her the leading question, but it was implicit. And by her tone, he knew there was more coming, so he waited. Working in a drapery was very different from working at Madame Chambon's.

Violet sighed and looked down at her lap. "You will think badly of me when I tell you the next part of my sorry tale."

CHAPTER 9

Max blinked and wished he hadn't. Whatever else she misread in his expression indicated that he already thought the worst of her. And he certainly didn't.

"Yet, Max, it gets worse. It wasn't as if I hadn't already sealed my fate. As if I hadn't already cast myself into the ranks of the impure. The fallen. I just hoped no one would discover my shame."

"I don't think you need to be so harsh on yourself. You were very young." Max stroked her heavy dark hair. It was soft and smooth and carefully coiled in the fashion of the day. Violet was an exquisite-looking woman. She'd have enjoyed a great deal of male interest, surely. Yet she'd had no guiding influence. Nor had Max, but he was a man. Mabel had reminded him of this often enough, teasing him about the way he muddled through life oblivious of the niceties sometimes, and that she wasn't sure she wanted to devote her life to teasing out his potential. She'd said it playfully during the past couple of years of their betrothal. Lord, they'd been on the verge of getting married so many times, but an untimely death or something else had always pushed back the date.

He stroked Violet's cheek. She was the one who needed guidance, and he didn't want to think about Mabel. "Obviously, you'd been taken advantage of by your grandmother's acquaintance. Your grandmother would hardly have spoken of it. I'm sure you needn't have worried."

Violet sent him a wry look. She continued, "It was heavy work and long hours. I didn't enjoy it. But there was one bright spot." She sighed but didn't smile. "A gentleman who seemed kind used to stop by the shop, first to buy ribbons for his nieces and then, after a while, he paid me compliments. When I'd known him for several weeks, he crossed my path on my way home and, as we were both heading into the same tearooms, he bought me tea and buns."

She squeezed her hands together and sent Max an imploring look. "You must understand how lonely I was. Apart from my weekly letter from Emily, I had nothing to look forward to. No other family and no friends, for Grandmother had discouraged friendships since we'd returned from India. Besides, I'd grown up in India, not England. I'd not gone to school here. Grandmother kept us isolated. I had no one."

"I understand, Violet. I shan't judge you harshly." He suspected he knew where her story was going and wished he didn't.

"One evening, when I'd known Cedric about two months, he invited me to the theatre. He bought me supper afterwards, and we had wine. He told me he loved me and kissed me. I thought I loved him too. It wasn't too hard to persuade me, when he was walking me back to my boarding house, to stop by his own lodgings. I hadn't had anyone tell me I meant anything to them in so long."

She stiffened in his arms as she brought the back of her

hand across her face. Max held her tighter. "I went with him to his bedroom. He hadn't made me drunk. I went of my own free will. I wanted human contact. I wanted to feel loved."

Her eyes were large and imploring. As if she really did want Max's exoneration. "Afterwards, as I lay in his arms, feeling happiness like a glow throughout my body, he said, "My sister told me you were a whore. And now I've proved it."

Max gasped. He'd not expected *this*. Unsure what to say, he held her as she stared over his shoulder and recounted her tale in a soft, unemotional voice.

"I cried as I put on my clothes and didn't stop as I ran all the way home, alone, in the dark. Two days later, my grand-mother wrote to say she was cutting off my allowance. She'd heard about my loose character from too many quarters, and it was clear I could survive well enough selling the commodity that only the virtuous quarantined for marriage. Those were her very words. I'll never forget them."

Max studied her pale, drawn, beautiful face. She was honest and she'd been badly used. He didn't know what to say, but he had to offer what comfort he could. "Then you were forced into this work. You had no choice." He wanted to exonerate her, but she wouldn't have it.

"I had a choice. I could have worked my fingers to the bone and perhaps, with time, I'd have managed to win the affections of a man who'd have me as an honest woman." She grimaced. "Lord knows, it's not possible to survive on the wage of a draper's assistant without learning the necessary economies that must support such a position. And even then, an unforeseen need for a doctor or pharmacist often meant there was not enough left of my wage to both put food on the table for the week *and* keep a roof over my head. What little I knew about money was that there was never enough of it. I was always late with the rent and constantly threatened with eviction. But you're wrong. I did have a choice. And I chose to present myself on Madame Chambon's doorstep the very next day because I'd heard her name spoken with the utmost contempt because she traded in Cyprians. Lightskirts. Barques of Frailty. Prostitutes. And that's what Cedric had said I was. Not only had he said it, but he'd proved it. I knew it in my heart, and now my grandmother knew it. I can't change my past. I am destined for hell and damnation; however, I still have some years on Earth which I would like to spend as pleasantly as possible. I have no intention of going to a nunnery to repent or throwing myself into thankless hard labour just to keep from starving. Women don't earn enough to keep themselves, and I'll not sell my body on a street corner for a few shillings just to keep ahead of the creditors. Lord Bainbridge is going to set me up. The arrangements have almost been finalised. Two weeks from now, after I have fulfilled my obligations to you, I shall leave Madame Chambon's to become Lord Bainbridge's mistress."

Max felt unaccountably discomposed. There was such bleakness in her tone. Her judgement of herself was so harsh and cold.

"Surely you could go back home? Your grandmother could not be so unfeeling as to refuse to take you in. And there's your sister. You need to think of her."

"My sister is dead."

She said it so flatly, yet the pain that flashed across her face was greater than that which she'd shown when recounting her own miserable situation.

He wasn't sure what to say.

"Emily died of typhoid last year. She's buried in the village of Ruislip which is where my grandmother lives and where I have no intention of ever returning. So, you see, I have no one to be good for." She smiled and touched his face. "And I am certainly not here to be good, Max." She rose, her delicate, long-fingered hands hovering at the buttons at her throat. "Please Max, I know you invited me here to prove you have scruples. But you didn't have to prove that for I already knew it, just as I know that in less than a week, there will be nothing more between us."

Max closed his eyes and tried to subdue the violent impulses that were warring within his breast and, quite as uncontrollably, in his groin. His whole being ached for this woman. For her touch, light and delicate upon his bare skin, that never failed to whip him into the most exquisite delight, a precursor to a myriad of intense sensations and ultimately devastating satisfaction that was the inevitable culmination.

She wanted this. It wasn't an act. He wasn't paying her extra. This was no additional bargain. It was simply a coming together through want and need.

And he needed it as much as she did. For she satisfied his need for closeness with a woman like no woman ever had. Being in her arms made him feel a sense of freedom and fulfilment he'd not felt before.

CHAPTER 10

*N*oon was far too early for Max to present himself to anyone. Certainly after the excesses of the night before. So, to discover that not only his grandfather, but his grandfather's old friend and neighbour, Lord Camberwell were awaiting him in his drawing room was a shock of the highest order.

Hesitating before the door, he wondered if he should make an ignominious exit through the scullery. Perhaps he could pay Violet a call.

Immediately he realised Violet was not available to him for such spontaneous visits. He'd have to gird his loins and face what he must without her.

Feeling unaccountably forlorn at the thought, he turned the doorknob and opened the door, pushing back his shoulders to face the occupants of the light and elegant, high-ceilinged room, who were currently engaged in drinking tea but who would soon focus their frighteningly incisive scrutiny upon himself.

"Hello Mabel," he said with commendable lack of irony as

he stepped forward to greet his errant would-be-bride. "This is a surprise."

She nodded her neatly coiffured head and fixed him with her intense green eyes, the most surprising feature in her pleasant, serene face, though there was nothing he could see that was precisely wrong with her mouth, which was turning up at the corners. Except that it completely failed to move him as did the full, soft, rosebud lips that belonged to Violet Lilywhite.

And as an image flashed through his mind of the violent sensations Miss Violet Lilywhite had evoked upon him during the three notable occasions this past fortnight that had changed his life, he reflected that he'd never actually kissed Mabel's lips.

Nor had he ever wanted to.

"Not an unpleasant one, I hope."

To his surprise, she rose and went towards him, stopping in the middle of the floor as she looked between Lord Granville and Max. "I think we need to talk, Max." She smiled an apology at Aunt Euphemia who, Max noted, looked as if she didn't know what to say, and his grandfather who reclined in his wingback chair looking like a kingmaker as he smiled upon the pair.

"Yes, Max. You and Mabel should enjoy the sunshine on this beautiful morning. Mabel has something to say to you." He patted his checked waistcoat, his iron-gray moustache twitching, signalling the smile he was trying to suppress.

And Max felt the dread seep up from the soles of his shoes as he added, "I think it will make you very happy."

It was afternoon by the time Violet opened her eyes and focused on the flock wallpaper of her small room.

The smell of burnt toast wafted through the cracks in the floorboards, and the chatter of girls and servants going about their business in the passage outside her room was mildly disturbing when all she wanted was silence.

She closed her eyes and hugged herself, imagining she was in Max's embrace and the pressure around her ribcage and breasts came from his strong arms.

Last night, she'd experienced every emotion to be had. There'd been the shame of confession; the brazenness of putting into words the baseness of what she wanted.

And then the sweet joy of fulfillment.

Max had been passionate. He'd been tender, and he'd been loving.

She'd felt loved, and that was what Violet had wanted. She'd not known if it was possible for her heart and soul to soak up another's emotion and to actually feel loved. She wouldn't question too hard whether that was manufactured on her part because it didn't matter. She didn't have to question whether Max would be around beyond next week, because she knew he wouldn't.

But he'd made her feel loved and cherished and desired last night, and that was all she'd required.

In a little over a week, Lord Bainbridge would move in to fulfil his role, and Violet would continue to have a roof over her head and good food to eat.

And really, wasn't that what life was all about?

Existing with the minimum amount of pain.

She rose and dressed in a plain, no-longer-fashionable striped day dress then went downstairs. Several of the girls, their hair unkempt, their eyes lacklustre with weariness, were sewing at the refectory table in the scullery. The modish gowns provided for the evenings were always carefully fitted and chosen, but a girl had to remodel her daywear from the secondhand offerings Madame kept in a wardrobe in the box room.

"That's a nice dress, Charity," she said, pouring herself tea from the teapot on the sideboard. "Did your young man buy it for you?"

Of all the girls at Madame Chambon's, Violet thought Charity the sweetest. The other girls obviously thought the same, for none of them regarded her with envy even though she was clearly the most fortunate of them all.

Violet could not imagine how wonderful it would be to have the loyalty of a man who was simply waiting until he was in a position to make her his own.

"Hugo has to go away."

As Violet seated herself at the table, a little distance away, she saw the girl's eyes were red-rimmed. "Going away?" Charity surely didn't mean for more than a few weeks. Charity and Hugo were simply biding their time until the young man came into his inheritance. "He'll be back," she said comfortingly, thinking of Max who really was going away forever. Or as close to that as made no difference. Her heart squeezed with pain.

"His father is sending him away to run his tea plantation in some faraway place across the sea I don't even want to think about." Charity put down her dress and rubbed her eyes. "I don't know that I'll ever see him again."

"Good lord!" Violet didn't know what to say. "I...I'm so sorry."

Charity managed a wan smile. "I shouldn't have expected the happy ending. Your young man is leaving in less than a week, too. But you shall be married, and I shall be your bridesmaid and that will make me very happy, Violet. I need something to cheer me. Something to look forward to."

"You know it's only a sham wedding to please his aunt." The words stuck in Violet's throat.

"I know. But you'll have that memory to cherish for the rest of your life." Charity rethreaded her needle and picked up her sewing again. "You never thought it was anything else."

Violet suspected Charity had harboured secret hopes that her fairy tale might have had an unconventional ending. That the baronet's son might really have wed the girl from the gutter.

She poured more tea, spilling some onto the threadbare tablecloth. She didn't bother to wipe it away. What was the point? Some stains were indelible. And even if the cloth was laundered, it would only gather more filth. Madame's concern for appearance was only skin-deep. As long as her girls looked their best for their gentleman admirers when they had their pocket books at the ready, she cared little for the rest.

"I will treasure the memory, Charity. Both Max and his aunt have been so very kind." She stood up suddenly, her voice choking on the words, and instantly Charity dropped her sewing and went to her. "Violet, I'm so sorry. I was thinking only of myself. Of course, you must have hoped for more. Don't we all?"

Violet shook her head. "I've learnt too much to hope that." She heaved in a breath, stepping blindly towards the door. She mustn't think so much of herself. She'd accepted the arrangement. There was no point in wishing for what she'd known could never happen. "Why is Hugo allowing his family to send him away?" she asked, stopping and forcing herself to focus on her friend's distress rather than her own.

Charity stared at the floor. At the two threadbare hems of the day dresses no gentleman would ever see them wear. Violet thought what a dispirited pair they must look and how no gentleman would find either of them the least bit entrancing in the morning gloom.

"He lost a lot of money at the card table." When she raised her eyes, she looked ashamed. "Hugo doesn't gamble as a rule. But he was put under a lot of pressure, and he believed he couldn't lose." She shrugged. "We all make mistakes and I forgive him but…" She let out a sob. "I don't know if I'll ever get over the grief of losing him." She put out her hand and gripped Violet's arm. "You're so strong, Violet. An inspiration. Truly you are. When Lord Belvedere raises your veil to kiss you in the church, *I* shall be the one to cry. You're so much stronger than I could ever be."

CHAPTER 11

With his hands thrust into his pockets and his shoulders hunched, Max headed into the wind at Mabel's side. A stiff breeze was blowing, whipping the trees and sending shivers down his spine. It was not walking weather but clearly, Mabel had something important to say.

Which Max was dreading.

Beneath a spreading oak, they stopped, and Max stared morosely into the murky river, wondering what dreadful thing Mabel would say.

"Well, here we are, alone at last, Max. You must be very angry with me."

He shrugged, glancing at her. "I wasn't sure what to think, to tell you the truth."

"Your grandfather was certainly angry, as was mine." She shifted a little so that she was standing right before him.

Max stared down at her, meeting her sparkling green eyes in her plain, pale face.

Her mouth turned up pertly. "Do you want to kiss me?"

The last thing he expected was her trill of laughter a

second later. "Oh, Max! What a dreadful actor you are. You should have seen the horror on your face. Now I *know* I did the right thing by leaving you standing at the altar. I just promised our grandfathers that I would do my best to patch things up between us." She rubbed her hands together to warm them in the cold. "I swore I would do all in my power to salvage whatever might be salvaged, and now I can confidently report back that nothing can be."

"I didn't mean to be rude or hurt your feelings," Max said gruffly. He didn't like being called a terrible actor when everything he'd been doing the past two weeks had been acting.

"Max, I've known you almost my whole life, and you are such a dear friend. I'd do anything for you, you know that, except make you marry me—even though you're probably the only offer I'm ever going to get."

"Now, don't say that, Mabel," he protested.

"Well, I've hardly garnered much interest from other male quarters, and we both can say quite honestly that I am no oil painting."

"You have the most beautiful eyes, and you're the kindest person, Mabel." He meant it. "I don't want to see you moulder away and bear the brunt of your grandfather's ire." Nor did he want to marry Mabel.

"Neither do I, but worse would be living with a man who is in love with somebody else." Mabel put up her hand to stop him speaking. "Your aunt spilled the beans before I'd even stated the reason for my visit. Poor Miss Thistlethwaite never looked more awkward in her life than when her brother started discussing the possibility of a match between us going ahead after all. So, do tell, Max; what does she look like, and how has she managed to capture your heart when no one else could?"

"I wouldn't say no one else—"

"Lord Max, you're notoriously hard to please. She must be very special indeed. What's her name?"

"Violet Lilywhite, and you're right; she is very special." Max found himself smiling just to speak of her. "She's very strong and brave, and she's also the most beautiful woman I've ever seen. She deserves someone who will give her only the best." He couldn't look Mabel in the eye as he added, "I'm not sure I'm that man, though."

"Well, you'll have to do what is required if she's already agreed to marry you" Mabel looked fit to burst with excitement. "So, clearly you've put aside that concern. Miss Thistlethwaite told me you're eloping. Don't worry; I've promised not to say a word, but it is rather thrilling news, you know, and not at all what I expected of you. Except that, now I think about it, you *would* fall for a woman who was beautiful, adventurous, and who needed you." She bit her lip. "Funny, when I put it like that, I'm none of those things, so I really should have come to my senses long before. But you, Max, you've been in love with her for some time, I gather? So, my non-appearance in church finally gave you the impetus to act and to follow your heart. Good on you, I say!"

Max ran a finger around the inside of his collar which was feeling far too tight. It seemed wrong to meet Mabel's enthusiasm with more lies. And yet, everything he'd said about Violet was true.

Mabel squeezed his hand. "Don't worry; your grandfather won't know a thing until it's all gone ahead, and you and Miss Lilywhite are safely married." She put her head on one side and considered her childhood friend. "Do you know Max, you look far too handsome in that unreliable, scoundrel-ish way that so many women do seem to fall for, and yet you are the most noble, honourable, dutiful man I know. Miss Lilywhite is a very lucky young woman."

A squall of light rain pelted them amidst the leaves

carried on the breeze and they both turned back to the house.

Max suddenly felt very humbled. "You know, Mabel, you deserve better. I hope you will be happy."

Her smile was confident as she tucked her hand into the crook of his arm, and they trod the damp grass up the small hill to the neat Georgian brick house where so much speculation would no doubt be going on inside. "I'm much happier now that I know I did the right thing," she said.

NOW BACK IN HER NEAT BLACK SKIRT AND BODICE, VIOLET FELT a different person as she trod the stairs at Miss Thistlethwaite's side for the final fitting of her wedding gown.

While they waited for Madame to emerge from the workroom beyond, the older lady could barely contain her excitement. "You will look radiant, my dear! I can't wait to see Max's face when he beholds his beloved looking like the answer to his dreams." Her hacking cough stopped Violet from telling her fondly what a dear, sentimental creature she was.

With some concern, she accompanied Madame to the changing room to be helped out of her garments and into the crackling ivory silk creation with its shimmering trimmings and its exquisite lace veil.

Even she gasped as she stepped in front of the looking glass in the large, lofty viewing chamber while everyone gazed on.

"My dear girl, I've never seen such a sight for sore eyes!" Miss Thistlethwaite exclaimed. "You are even more the beauty. How I shall miss you." She brightened. "However, it'll only be for a few short months. I am determined I shall still be around when you return from your wedding tour so I can hear how you enjoyed Venice. How I longed to visit Venice when I had the strength."

Violet managed a smile. How she hated this escalation of lies. What had started out as a means of gratifying Max's beloved aunt was turning into an increasingly cumbersome charade.

Unable to answer, she kept her gaze trained on her reflection. The intricately embroidered and pleated train was a dashing counterpoint to the low, lace-edged neckline, while the sculpted bodice with its 19-inch waist would be a reminder of Violet's heyday. She had to regard the striking image before her in these terms for Max was not the one being pleased here. This was an extravagant show for Miss Thistlethwaite's benefit.

Funded by Miss Thistlethwaite.

"You've become very dear to me these past two weeks." The old lady raised her hand and touched Violet's cheek while she supported herself with the other on one of the bolts of fabric lining the walls of the room. "You're a good girl, Violet, and Max deserves you. I know you'll be happy together just as I knew in my heart that he and Mabel weren't suited, for all that I love Mabel like a daughter."

She coughed again, and Violet regarded her with concern. Miss Thistlethwaite had taken Violet on trust. Out of the goodness of her heart, she had transformed Violet, believing only the best.

And all the while the old lady was dying.

Violet closed her eyes while acid stung the back of her throat, and a wave of self-revulsion powered through her. No, Max didn't deserve her, and Miss Thistlethwaite certainly didn't deserve to be taken advantage of by a money-grubbing street girl.

Violet could hardly describe herself any better than that

"Why, Violet; you're as sentimental as I am. Look at those

tears in your eyes." Miss Thistlethwaite sent her a watery smile. "I will have to decide whether you are crying for happiness at becoming Max's wife or pleasure at seeing how beautiful you look."

The irony of her pronouncement was too much for Violet. With as much dignity as she could muster, she practised an elegant sashay about the room while she struggled for words.

"I don't deserve any of this, Miss Thistlethwaite," she said eventually, when she'd come to a stop in front of her benefactress. Helplessly, she skimmed her sides with her hands, delicately touching her fine veil with its rich edging of lace. "You have been so very kind and there's no way I can repay you—"

"Please, Violet; I did nothing that wasn't to please myself. I'm only glad that I've been able to bring happiness to those I love most in this life."

She looked so distressed that Violet knew it was pointless to go on. In two days, she and Max would meet secretly at the little church, where his aunt and Charity would be waiting as witnesses, for the marriage that was designed solely to give Max his freedom, and his dying aunt a moment of pleasure and relief.

Violet felt very burdened by her secret knowledge though it was some small consolation that, in truth, Miss Thistlethwaite could hardly take her money to the next world. Nor was Violet benefitting financially from her largesse, she had to remind herself. She'd not own the beautiful gown. Much as she might like to possess such an exquisite garment, it would feel like stealing if she secreted it away with her to Madame Chambon's. For where else could she keep it? Madame Chambon would purloin it the moment Violet brought it inside, and she could hardly ask Lord Bainbridge to safeguard it for her until such time as he'd formalised the offer he'd agreed to. No, not even then, for Violet needed her own little bower to keep her things safe.

Dear lord, it was all so sordid.

"Please, Violet; you are happy, aren't you?"

Miss Thistlethwaite's anxious question intruded and Violet turned, forcing her eyes to shine with some emotion that would give her the comfort she needed.

"I am happy. Who could not be wild with happiness if they were to be marrying Max before the week is out? I must be patient, mustn't I, Miss Thistlethwaite. I suppose I keep worrying that something will go wrong."

Immediately she wished she hadn't said it for that only put the fear into Miss Thistlethwaite's own delicate breast.

"Don't you fear on that score, my dear. If my brother got wind of this, I would fight for your happiness as I never did for my own. I'm no longer the timid dormouse I once was but a fearsome proponent of the love match, believe me!"

Violet smiled at her fierce pronouncement, and was still smiling as she and Miss Thistlethwaite made their companionable way home, enjoying the fine weather to take a detour through Green Park.

Her past fears dissipated with the grey clouds that had accompanied them to her fitting. Miss Thistlethwaite truly did find real pleasure in her little exercise and, as long as it was sanctioned by Max, what did it matter that they wouldn't go ahead with it? Violet had done nothing wrong other than agree to what Max had proposed.

Max. She tried to banish his image from her mind.

"Just stop a moment. I think I'll sit down for a bit."

Violet turned and saw that Miss Thistlethwaite was holding her side; her breathing laboured. She helped settle the old lady on a park bench. Couples strolled companionably through the park; children played by the water's edge, and ducks quacked nearby. Everyone looked supremely contented as Violet scanned her fellow park dwellers. However, even as the old lady got her breath, her grey pallor was troubling.

"Home is less than five minutes' walk. I'll be right as rain in just a minute." Miss Thistlethwaite tried but failed to sound light and unconcerned.

Violet heard the clock chiming the hour, and her anxiety grew. She needed to be back at Madame Chambon's now, and Madame was a stickler for timekeeping.

Miss Thistlethwaite misinterpreted the extent of Violet's concern. "You have your work to go to, my dear. Just leave me. I can make my own way back. Truly I can."

It was tempting. Violet hesitated as she weighed up whether to make her way directly towards Soho or to see Miss Thistlethwaite all the way home. But the old lady's hacking cough made up her mind.

"I'm going to fetch someone," she said, panicked suddenly by the flecks of blood she saw on Miss Thistlethwaite's handkerchief. The sun had gone behind a cloud, and the temperature had plummeted in just the past five minutes. She wished she had something warmer to put around Miss Thistlethwaite's shoulders.

Hurrying towards the crescent of townhouses where Max lived and that was, fortunately, only a few blocks away, she felt her own heartbeat begin to race. Max would hardly be pleased if she showed her face in his respectable drawing room for what he might consider a flimsy excuse.

She could, perhaps, leave a note.

But what if there was a delay and Miss Thistlethwaite was left waiting even five minutes longer than she need be.

When she reached the black wrought-iron railings of the handsome, white-painted dwelling, Violet wasn't sure whether to take the stairs down to the servants' basement entrance or knock boldly on the front door.

She swallowed nervously as the deferential nod of the butcher's boy decided her. If he considered her good enough to enter by the front door, she was not going to join him on the journey below. She was dressed neither as a whore nor a servant. She'd be received by the butler; she was sure of it.

Two minutes later, with that ordeal behind her, she waited in even more trepidation as the parlourmaid knocked on the drawing room door to announce her.

And she was fully braced for Max's surprise—or was it shock?—when she was admitted.

What she wasn't expecting, however, was to become the focus of not just Max, but an elderly gentleman and a plain but pleasant-faced young woman.

"Forgive me the intrusion, but I am a friend of Miss Thistlethwaite," she explained, before elaborating on the nature of her visit. "I couldn't leave her alone, unattended, without seeking someone's assistance, yet I have another important engagement I must meet."

She glanced at Max when she said this and saw the telltale clench of his jaw. He knew exactly what she meant, and she suddenly longed for him to stride across the room and take her in his arms before declaring to the gathering that he'd decided to make her his wife.

In name, *and* in reality.

Of course, it didn't happen. However, he did thank her, and then announced to the man whom she was not surprised to learn was his grandfather, and to Miss Dulwich—whom she was certain was the infamous Mabel—that he'd accompany Miss Lilywhite to his aunt.

"That was a clever way of garnering my attention," he remarked when they were alone and walking briskly towards the park, though it seemed Max didn't believe Violet was motivated by concern for his aunt until she told him she really did have to go.

The furrows between his eyes deepened. "I thought this was a ploy for us to be together." He sounded genuinely disappointed.

Violet laughed as she pointed towards the gated park. "Go to your aunt, Max. She needs someone to help her back home, and I can assure you Madame Chambon would not think that a good enough excuse to keep me from earning her the diamonds and furs needed to add to her consequence."

Her tone was light, but the set to Max's mouth was grim as he suddenly gripped her hands.

"I care for you, Violet," he muttered. "Is there nothing I can do to help you escape that dreadful woman's clutches?"

"You're marrying me tomorrow." Violet strove for lightness as she tossed back the thick brown ringlet that fell over her shoulder. "And you're paying me well for it. Now, good night and send my good wishes to Miss Thistlethwaite for I should have been at Madame Chambon's ten minutes ago."

CHAPTER 12

Max was glad to find only the ladies when he returned to the townhouse for the old men had left for their club. It was, he decided, a good sign. If they'd suspected anything between Violet and himself, his grandfather would have had no compunction in grilling him on it in front of everyone.

"Miss Lilywhite is very lovely, Max," Mabel remarked with a sly look as he accepted the tea she poured him. "Where did you meet her?"

"At a mutual friend's establishment. She is a very modern young lady and believes a chaperone unnecessary since she works for her living." It was easy to trot out the lines he had ready. Not so easy when Mabel asked him, "Are you very much in love with her?"

He barely knew what to say, and Mabel laughed when he had to tip the tea from his saucer back into his teacup.

"I hope you're less clumsy as an escort," Mabel said. "Miss Lilywhite looks as regal as a queen. I can't believe she has not been snapped up already and must work for her living."

"My understanding is that her family hails from Middle-sex. Ruislip, I believe."

Max sent a sharp look at his aunt. "She is estranged from them," he said quickly, "and they will not be coming to the secret ceremony."

"Ceremony!" Mabel gasped. "Why Max, you sly thing! You're going to elope? Goodness, your grandfather—"

"Must not suspect," he shot back.

Mabel's sudden blush and Aunt Euphemia's evasive look prompted him to ask suspiciously, "They made no remark about my accompanying Miss Lilywhite part way home? I'd have made such an offer to any unaccompanied young lady; they must surely know that." Nervously, he straightened his collar. "You won't say anything, will you, Mabel?"

"Of course not." She bit her lip and nodded vigorously. "I'm sure everything will be fine, Max."

"At least I know Miss Lilywhite will not leave you at the altar, my dear boy."

"No, I don't anticipate it." He only realised that the senti-ment might be misinterpreted by Mabel when his old friend said, "And I have done you the greatest service, Max, and will do everything in my power that you win the love match you deserve."

His aunt sighed. "If ever there was a young lady in love." Her voice trailed off, and she dabbed her eyes.

It was hard not to be affected by Aunt Euphemia's emotion, which was touching, and Max had to admit it, curi-ously painful. But while he'd set out to please her, and it was gratifying to see her vicarious pleasure in helping facilitate a happiness she'd never experienced, Max felt a scoundrel for duping her.

"Really, Aunt, I think Violet could have found herself a much better catch than me." He was embarrassed. Not only was he cheating his aunt, but he was also cheating Violet. Yes, she'd agreed with the terms. But that was then.

So much had changed.

~

"What a splendid looking young woman."

Lord Granville accepted the tea Euphemia handed to him while she tried to keep her expression impassive before attempting to turn the topic. She was not quick enough.

But suddenly, there was Mabel making things a great deal worse.

"Did you see the way Max looked at her? He certainly never looked at me like that, Grandfather." Mabel turned an appealing look towards the door as her grandfather entered the room. When Euphemia had been surprised by the unannounced arrival of the two elderly friends who'd had travelled down from the country together, she'd been right to fear the worst. Neighbours for more than fifty years, they had always been set upon a match between their respective grandchildren. She shifted in her seat, her expression combative. Mabel was docile so much of the time but when she dug in her heels, she was the most stubborn creature Euphemia had ever met. She both admired and abhorred this trait in the girl she'd known all her life. Sometimes Mabel was her own worst enemy.

"It's why I refused him," Mabel went on in a self-righteous tone that would set up the bristles of the two elderly gentlemen, Euphemia was certain. "I believe that in 1878 it's not unreasonable to desire a love match. I think of Max more like a brother than a potential husband."

If ever there was an occasion when Euphemia wished young Mabel was as discreet as she was usually in the presence of her elders, it was now.

"Admiration is one thing. Choosing a suitable mate requires a great deal more than that."

It was Septimus who answered, and his look was not nearly as indulgent as it had been. His beetling grey eyebrows jutted over his bulbous pale-blue eyes as he turned towards his sister. "Tell me, Euphemia; what do you know of Miss Lilywhite?"

Euphemia began to shake under the glare of his scrutiny, though she tried hard not to let her usual fear show. Septimus had an uncanny knack of ferreting out her weak spots, making her gabble all sorts of indiscretions through pure terror.

She pressed her lips together. Not this time. No, she would not reveal anything that would jeopardise Max's chance at happiness.

Unable to meet his eye, she said in a tone barely above a whisper, "It's true she works for her living, but she is a good, honest young woman who has fallen on difficult times." She forced herself to concentrate on her hands in her lap rather than his face. The hardness of his gaze would undo her; she knew. Her throat felt swollen as she tried to push out the words with a false lightness. "I don't know that Max knows her at all."

"But isn't she—?" Mabel put her hands to her lips before the words were out, causing Septimus to narrow his eyes as he swivelled his head in her direction.

"Isn't she what?"

Now it was Mabel's grandfather who was demanding filial obedience. "What do you know that you're not telling us, Mabel?" He was like Septimus. Uncompromising. Demanding. A man who expected a dutiful granddaughter as Septimus expected a dutiful sister.

And grandson.

And that's why it was so important that Euphemia not be

the faulty cog that consigned Max's hopes of happiness to cinders.

"I'm sure I wasn't going to say anything." Mabel's feigned innocence was even more jarring in the tense atmosphere. For Mabel knew not the first thing about lying, and it showed. "Max has said nothing, he's only intimated…I mean, when he said he couldn't marry me, it wasn't because there was anyone else and certainly not Miss Lilywhite…"

She was gabbling now, making things worse, just as Euphemia might have had she lost her nerve. Mabel knew it, and Euphemia knew she knew it, but the girl was unpractised and as terrified of her male guardian as Euphemia was of hers.

"Euphemia."

Septimus's tone was low and quiet, but it reverberated around the drawing room like a foghorn in the horrified stillness broken only by the rattle of Euphemia's teacup against the saucer in her trembling hands.

"Yes, Septimus." She could barely get the words out. She was cowering; she knew. And Mabel was looking on in horror as if Euphemia really was about to receive a lashing. Abject creature that she was. The self-loathing was like a living organism, slithering through her body, threatening to choke her.

"Miss Lilywhite is a friend of yours, she says? An unusual type of friend for someone such as you, Sister. I wonder if perhaps you have helped facilitate an even more unusual friendship between my grandson and the young lady?" He waited. And when Euphemia didn't answer, her silence seemed to corroborate his apparent suspicions. With chilling import, he went on, "And I wonder what else you might have facilitated between the young lady if Max is suddenly so anxious to separate himself from our worthy Mabel, whom he was to have married only three short weeks ago."

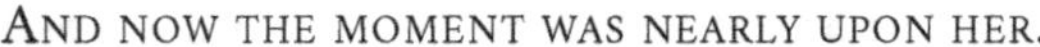

AND NOW THE MOMENT WAS NEARLY UPON HER.

Her marriage.

Her sham marriage.

Violet stared miserably at her veiled reflection, immune to the gasps of admiration from the girls who gathered round her in Madame Chambon's reception room.

Even Madame Chambon was suitably impressed.

"The first bride I've ever despatched to anyone better than the butcher's boy, my girl. You've done well even if it is a sham wedding." She rubbed her hands together, and Violet imagined her doing the same thing in the solitude of her study as she ran gold coins through her fingers.

It had been impossible to conceal the transaction, though initially, Violet had tried. However, Miss Thistlethwaite's numerous requests for fittings and other requests to Miss Violet Lilywhite at 56 Albemarle St could not be kept secret for long.

Madame got her cut on every transaction made by her girls, meaning the pecuniary rewards from the contract Violet had made were considerably diluted. It was true that Max had transferred funds directly into an account set up in her name, but Madame was not stupid. She'd calculated her due, even if she wasn't aware of the exact amount Max had paid Violet.

Which meant it was just as well Violet had Lord Bainbridge's offer to fall back on when Max was out of her life.

A thought that made her heart cleave and tears spring unbidden to her eyes.

Foolish girl. She'd known love could never be her destiny the moment she'd thrown away her reputation. Well, the moment she'd presented herself at Madame Chambon's. She just hadn't expected to feel so much.

"You'll be the only one of us who ever takes away a wedding dress as your best memory of working here," remarked Charity wistfully. "But perhaps you really will persuade Lord Belvedere to make an offer that occasions donning the beautiful creation. For *real,* I mean, when he sees how beautiful you look."

This brought both sighs and snickers from the other girls, but for Violet, it was only another reminder of how bleak her future really was. Lord Bainbridge, not Lord Belvedere, would keep her in the short term, and he was not a man for whom she had a particular liking. He was mercurial and viewed their relationship in terms of a transaction that was solely to his benefit. No doubt for as long as Violet was pleasing and kept her looks. Violet was, after all, only a whore.

With a sigh, she turned back from the mirror while the girls who'd crowded around parted to let her make her way to the bed where she'd laid out her black cloak. Charity helped her into it and, carefully, she drew the hood over her veil and smoothed the concealing folds of her exquisite silk confection.

"Are you ready, Charity?" she asked.

"Are *you* ready, Violet?" asked one of the girls. "I don't expect you back tonight. You look a proper princess ripe for kidnapping."

"You'd better come back as you've not accounted for all that you owe me," Madame Chambon warned, putting her hand on Violet's shoulder before offering her a rare compliment. "You look beautiful, Violet, and Lord Belvedere is a fool if he doesn't want to see me and negotiate a settlement. But yes, I know the story. The foolish boy thinks he needs to sow his wild oats in Africa in a bid to untie himself from his grandfather's apron strings. See if you can persuade him otherwise, Violet."

But Violet knew she could not. Regardless of how entranced Max might be with her, and consider her a vision from paradise tonight, he would be boarding a ship for Cape Town in a couple of days, and Violet knew there was nothing she, or anyone else, could do to persuade him otherwise.

Sadly, though with beating heart nevertheless, she walked the short distance from the house to the hackney where it was waiting on the damp cobblestones, horses snorting and breath steaming in the cold and swirling fog.

Yes, a common hackney cab for her sham marriage to a young lord with a heart full of kindness and a soul that dreamt of adventure.

Sham marriage. What a detestable term, she thought as the jarvey helped first Violet, then Charity, into the sour-smelling interior.

"Reckon I'm about to drive London's most beautiful ladies to meet their hearts' desires," he remarked as he slammed the door and tightened his muffler.

Which Violet thought was rather ironic and bittersweet under the circumstances.

"Is your heart beating as painfully as mine?" Charity whispered after a few minutes of silence. "Our hearts' desires," she repeated with a sigh. "We could imagine it was so."

Violet heard the effort it took the girl not to cry and the hitch in her voice as she went on, "We could pretend, just for a few minutes, that we really were within reach of all we ever wanted. Couldn't we?"

In the dim, waxy yellow light, Charity looked so much younger than her years. She'd lived at Madame Chambon's for more than eighteen months, but she'd known only the faithful love of one man. Until now, she'd been a symbol of hope and optimism, but with her future looking suddenly as bleak as Violet's, the wistfulness in her voice was heart-breaking.

Violet could endure but could Charity, who was about to be thrown to the wolves? Only the previous night, the detestable cousin of Charity's young man had swept into the brothel demanding that he be pleasured by 'Hugo's fancy piece'. Violet didn't know whether it was kindness on Madame's part, or the consideration that Charity might give better value if she were broken in by someone less vulgar and obviously drunk as Mr Algernon Black, but Charity had been given her reprieve. Tonight, she was accompanying Violet to say her meaningless vows. Another reprieve.

But what about tomorrow?

She clasped Charity's hand and pretended, for what was the harm? "Lord Belvedere would be a catch, even if he *were* the butcher's boy. He understands me, and he loves me, and tonight he's marrying me, despite the opposition of his grandfather." She forced a smile. "Doesn't that prove how much he loves me? That he'd oppose even his grandfather and risk family opprobrium for the sake of true love?"

"He does love you." Charity's voice was low and fierce "And don't you believe otherwise. I saw it in his eyes. That very first night. The way he looked at you wasn't the way most men look at the girls at Madame's." She shook her head. "There was real admiration there. He thought you the most splendid creature to cross his orbit. And even if he isn't really marrying you, he would if he could. If he were not Lord Granville's grandson."

Violet laughed and leaned back against the squabs, releasing the girl's hand to wipe an errant tear from the corner of her eye. "Darling Charity, you are the sweetest girl I know." She looked fondly at her friend. "You have a good heart, and you deserve only the very best. I am beyond redemption but you...you are still within reach of your happy ever after. You heard the girls at breakfast gossiping that their gentlemen admirers said Hugo had been tricked? Well, doesn't that bear investigation, for if it's found to be true, then the villain will be unmasked in time for you and Hugo to be together before he leaves to run his uncle's land-holdings across the sea." She felt suddenly very protective and very determined. "If I can't get my hearts' desire, Charity, I shall do everything within my power to ensure that you do."

With a lurch, the carriage drew up in front of a dark, squat building, shrouded in fog. The ghostly substance seemed to snake its way into the carriage as the door was opened from the outside.

Right into Violet's bones. She tried to stop herself shivering and, for a moment, even the comforting pressure of Charity's hand on her shoulder wasn't enough to propel her forward.

"It's all right, Violet. He's waiting for you inside. It's only a bat," Charity whispered as Violet cried out.

A single lantern hung by the entrance to the church door. The whole place looked very dark and forbidding.

"Now, take a deep breath. That's right. And one more."

With Charity's steady, soothing influence, Violet managed to ward off her last-minute reluctance. She didn't want to be part of what now seemed a hoax more cruel to herself than anything else.

Yet, even as she took two more steps towards the Greystone church, something didn't feel right. Why was everything in such darkness? Where was Max? There was no carriage; no welcoming light from within.

The clopping hooves and creaking harness of another equipage sounded unnaturally loud in the eerie silence as a hansom cab rounded the corner, coming to a halt beside them.

Max?

Violet ran the tip of her tongue over dry lips and prayed that he would step outside. Just to see his dear face would be a comfort, even with the knowledge their contact tonight would be fleeting.

And final.

"Miss Lilywhite."

Charity gripped Violet's hand, the two girls drawing back against the hackney as the unfamiliar voice issued from the lowered window. It was a woman's voice but its owner, heavily veiled, remained shadowed in the interior. "I came to warn you."

There was a definite waver towards the end of her words. Without waiting for Violet to reply, the woman went on breathlessly, "Max isn't coming. He can't. I'm so sorry, but his grandfather learnt of his plans."

Now her head emerged from the half-open window and she raised her veil. "Do you recognise me now? We met at Max's. Miss Dulwich." Her green eyes looked luminous in the damp light and her demeanour more agitated as she fingered her gloves.

Violet waited for her to go on.

So Max wasn't going to make it to his wedding after all. She looked down at her white silk slippers peeking from her froth of skirts and felt sad that he'd not see her looking like this after all.

"I'm so sorry," she said again. "You see, it was my fault. Lord Granville tricked me into telling him about your secret wedding, but now I'm here to atone. I had to take a detour on my way home after dinner so I have but seconds; only, you must know how much Max must love you if he's prepared to risk his grandfather's ire to marry you."

Violet blinked. What was the girl about? She surely couldn't believe the elopement was real?

"You must hurry, Miss Lilywhite, so Lord Granville doesn't discover you when he gets here. I sent him to St Patrick's, but the diversion won't keep him from discovering the truth before long." She leaned further out of the window and her large green eyes flashed with excitement in the carriage lamps. "Max is waiting for you at St Mary's." She pointed while her other hand clasped her breast. "Oh, but it is just too thrilling that Max is finally doing something so *worthwhile* and to please himself, for once. He's been so dutiful his whole life—right up to the point of marrying me. I knew I'd be the ruin of him, even though I would have been content enough—and, indeed, the envy of so many. But, at last, he's following his heart." She brushed aside a feather from her headdress that was stirred by the breeze and added as she began to withdraw her head, "I wish you great happiness, Miss Lilywhite, and I'm confident you will find it with Max. He's loyal to a fault and he adores you. I was quite satisfied on that score when I quizzed him." Hesitating, she smiled and put out her hand, grasping Violet's quickly when, bemused, Violet held hers out. "Hurry now...and I look forward to meeting you under less fraught conditions when you return from your wedding tour. You are very blessed to have found a man like Max. Good night."

Miss Dulwich tucked her head back into her carriage which gave a lurch before setting off down the road.

Charity had already given the jarvey directions, so Violet simply lay back against the squabs and awaited her fate while she tried not to cry.

For Miss Dulwich's words of hope and happiness were like cruel barbs.

By the time Violet entered St Mary's with Charity in

her wake, Miss Dulwich's hopeful sentiments were screaming at her. Falling in love with Max was the most ill-advised thing she'd ever done, now that she had so much to lose. When she'd agreed to his well-intentioned plan to please his aunt, Violet had had nothing to lose.

Now her heart beat painfully as she raised her head at an emotional gasp from Miss Thistlethwaite, seated in a front pew, and glimpsed Max over her shoulder, waiting for her at the end of the aisle, the priest behind him.

"My dear girl, you are a vision," the old lady whispered as Violet made her way down the worn runner, and the dewy look in Miss Thistlethwaite's pale-blue eyes made it clear that she was seeing in Violet the symbol of her own thwarted hopes and dreams. She put out her hand to grip Violet's wrist tightly, whispering, "You will make each other so happy. I feel it in my very soul."

Violet's throat swelled and her heart grew even heavier, for in deceiving Miss Thistlethwaite, she feared she was losing her last shreds of integrity. She was being paid for this, and wasn't it true that Violet only ever got paid when she lied?

"You look beautiful." Max looked as starstruck as his aunt as he gazed down at Violet when she arrived at his side, Charity just behind her. "A vision, like my aunt says." He stroked her cheek, and the genuine fondness in his gaze meant Violet had to blink away the tears.

"Thank you." What else was there to say? Perhaps Max was doing his best, and for his aunt's benefit, to appear every bit as smitten as Miss Thistlethwaite would have wanted him to look but Violet fancied his words came from the heart.

And for a few moments, she fancied that the actor before them really was a priest as he performed the ceremony that would have bound Violet and Max together, forever, under the law and in the eyes of the church.

"I do," she vowed, echoing Max's own promise when prompted, her hand clasped in his large, safe, warm hand.

She gazed up at him, recognised the genuine regret in his eyes and turned her head away to smile at Miss Thistleth-waite, who was sobbing happily in the front pew.

"My dearest Max, you could not have made me happier," the old lady declared between hiccupping intakes of breath. "Why, never have I seen two young people more in love and suited to one another than you."

CHAPTER 13

*M*ax was caught off guard. In the lamplight, Violet's pale skin had the lustre of alabaster, and her hair the sheen of a raven's wing. He didn't think he'd ever seen a woman so beautiful. There was a glow about her. She was the fulfillment of every husband-to-be's fantasy.

But that was not what he'd signed up for.

As he returned her limpid gaze, he imbued his look with all the longing and loving he felt in that moment. He could give free rein to his natural impulses for there was no need to act—yet, act he must, for Aunt Euphemia's sake.

It was regrettable that Mabel had become embroiled in his deception. His aunt was declining. It pained him to hear her wracking cough get the better of her with increasing frequency these days. Sometimes he found her in her chair, almost unresponsive to his welcome; she was so fatigued by a bout of coughing.

His aunt, he feared, would not live to discover his lie but Mabel would know, of course.

He didn't know if she'd be more shocked at the kind of woman Violet really was or at his elaborate deception.

Yet, gazing at Violet now, she could have passed muster as a princess, she looked so noble and angelic.

The priest's words sounded muted and unreal as Max obeyed his directive to kiss the bride.

His bride.

Gently he raised her veil and lowered his face to her soft, inviting lips.

VIOLET MELTED AT HIS TOUCH. THE BRUSH OF HIS LIPS AGAINST hers was like a butterfly's wing, tantalising and fleeting. He could risk no more.

But he did. And the sensation of desire it evoked was like warm honey flowing through her veins.

By the time Max and Violet drew apart, Miss Thistlethwaite was weeping delicately in the front pew, and Violet felt she would follow any minute.

In fact, her own eyes were wet as Max bent to kiss his aunt who was twisting her lace handkerchief in excitement.

It was late in the evening, and light snow covered the ground as they headed out towards the carriage.

"I hope I shall see you when you return from your wedding tour but if not, you know my heart has been gladdened more by this than anything else in my long and wasted life." She blinked rapidly. "For I have seen my dearest nephew allied with a woman he deserves."

Violet swallowed as she felt the pressure of Max's hand over hers and then a sudden panic.

What now? They'd not discussed what happened immediately after the ceremony. Throughout it all, Violet had hardened her heart using every ounce of physical willpower she had to be immune to feeling.

She'd blocked her ears to the words the priest was intoning, forcing the right expression only. Strangely, that part hadn't been too difficult to navigate when she'd feared it would be the most painful. However, she was so used to cauterising her feelings in the day to day—or evening to evening—rituals of her job that it came naturally.

Now, the expectation in Miss Thistlethwaite's expression as she saw them to their carriage made her suddenly ill with nerves while the greatest sense of loss swept through her like an icy blast. Max would gaze lovingly at her for the seconds it took to exit out of his aunt's line of vision, and then he'd direct the coachman to take her right back to Madame Chambon's.

It was all part of the arrangement, in theory.

"So, Max, I know discretion is of the utmost importance, but I hope you've found a lovely place to take Violet to tonight," his aunt murmured, causing Violet to blush. "She should get used to her new status as a wife before you embark on the excitement of travels."

"Indeed, it is all taken care of, Aunt."

Violet couldn't believe he responded so smoothly. None of the awkwardness of being caught on the back foot that she'd have exhibited.

"And where might this place be?" Violet asked as the carriage lurched forward. "You with your fine morals and fear of discovery will surely want to end this while you're ahead." Her voice sounded unaccountably bitter to her own ears.

She couldn't see him when he answered, but there was compassion in his voice.

"Friends as we've become cannot take each other's leave so coldly, Violet."

"I thought you couldn't wait to put a line under our little association. I'm hardly something to be proud of. You're an honourable man, Max. You don't consort with whores."

"I don't and I'm proud of it."

She found her hand encased in his in the dark. "And I don't consider you one." His voice was like a caress, but it did not change the fact that theirs was a transaction which supposedly took no account of hearts. "Regardless of how you make a living." His tone changed. Brightened.

Was he afraid Violet might get the wrong idea?

He patted her hand and leaned back against the squabs. "So now we're going to say a proper goodbye. I'm going to Africa in a few days, and you're going to surrender yourself to Lord Bainbridge. I'm jealous; I admit it, but I need to make my own way in the world, and you've known that from the start. I've not deceived you, have I?"

She shook her head. How could he speak so lightly?

"But you are not yet his, and I, like you, owe my allegiance to no one at this very moment. So, let us take our leave as we would want to. Like the friends we are."

Like the friends we are?

Despite the lump in Violet's throat, she wasn't sure she could manage saying goodbye at all if he insisted on this. But she could hardly admit her susceptibility. And there was no question about it being a goodbye forever. It was, and she might as well take what pleasure she could from it. She'd had precious little of that over the past few years.

So, with a smile for him as they passed into the light, turning into a better-lit part of town, she took the arm he offered when they alighted and tried to adopt a carefree tone as he led her up the path to the small guesthouse in Hampstead to which his carriage conveyed them.

Shaking out her skirts, she arranged the flounces of her bustle with care as they paused on the top step. "With rose petals in my hair and wearing such a dress as this, I don't think they'll look at us askance."

To her surprise, he put his hands on her shoulders. His

tone was warm. "You look every bit the bride I would consider the most beautiful in the world."

Except my corrupted soul prevents this becoming reality. But there was no point in spoiling the happy moment, Violet thought as she bit her lip, smiling back at him.

"The wife you choose will be a very lucky woman. You'll not throw yourself away lightly. Not as I have done," she added with a laugh and a quick squeeze of Max's arm to ameliorate the seriousness of her words. "I mean, in every instance but this one."

It was enough to defuse the tension so that both were smiling with real pleasure as they made themselves known to the landlady and signed the register.

Smiling. Like the happy, carefree newlyweds she assumed them to be.

THE ROOM WAS LARGE AND ELEGANTLY FURNISHED. VIOLET threw out her arms and twirled in the centre of the soft cream carpet, staring at the small chandelier above.

"What a palace," she declared, filled suddenly with pleasure and anticipation for what lay before her. A night of love and rapture. A final goodbye. She wouldn't be sad. She'd had more consideration shown her by this man than had ever come her way in a lifetime.

And she had the comfort of knowing Miss Thistlethwaite was content.

"And you are its queen." Max arrested her twirling as he caught her in his arms. "By God, I think I'm going to miss you, Miss Violet Lilywhite."

"For the duration of the journey to Cape Town, I daresay," she said, lightly. "I hope you suffer terribly on the voyage, and that Cape Horn is as rough as can be. I hope you think only of me as you retch miserably, knowing I shall be even more miserable at the knowledge that you found the prospect of shooting lions and tigers more diverting than me."

"Only lions, my dear, and I shall have to agree with you otherwise there'd be no point in this." He escorted her to the small, elegant sofa in front of the fireplace. "Let us make the most of our last night together. Of course, I shall miss you terribly. But the diversions of Africa beckon and the enticements are strong and..." he broke off "...the champagne has arrived."

A young maid entered following a tentative knock, bearing a tray with a bottle and two glasses.

"Now, let us drink to the future."

Violet was quiet as he carefully filled both their glasses. It seemed a cruel choice of words. What future did he think she had to look forward to?

But what was the point in spoiling it? If she'd learnt nothing else, it was to take the best that was on offer. "To the future," she said, tipping back her head and drinking deeply before brandishing her glass ready to be refilled. Perhaps another would help stop her from feeling.

Feeling too much pain at their impending separation.

Feeling too much pleasure at what would be their last time.

"And to you achieving splendid things, Max darling. Now, for goodness sake, enough of all this skirting about what we're really here for. Kiss me. Properly."

She was more than ready for the press of his soft, eager lips upon hers as he swept her into a tight embrace. With one hand clasping her waist, the other cupped her cheek as he savoured her response. She sighed with pleasure as he breached the seam of her lips, his tongue sweeping across her teeth, gaining access to the cavern of her mouth.

Her breasts tingled, and her belly roiled with need. No man had ever had this effect on her.

"Take me to bed, Max." Her whisper was hoarse with desire, but although the passion of his kiss gave her no reason to doubt he was as eager as she was to feel her skin against his, his response was tempered.

"Not too fast, my darling. I want to savour you."

She drew back slightly, surprised at the intensity of his look.

He dropped his hands. "Can I see you undress for me, Violet?" he whispered. "We've shared so much, but I want this to remember. I want to see what you look like."

How extraordinary that a whore could feel embarrassment at such a request. But whores were required to do as they were asked by the men who paid them.

He must have seen the reflection of such a sentiment flash across her face, for the moment she started unbuttoning her cuirass, he put a hand on her wrist to stay her.

"Only if you would do it willingly, though." He pressed his lips together as if he were anxious he'd offended her. "Only if you'd do it for a man you…"

He seemed to struggle for the words, and, with amusement, she supplied, "For a man you love?" She drew in a breath that forced up her breasts and slowly began to work on the row of tiny buttons at her front, as she smiled at him.

"Say if you want me to hasten the process. I'd hate you to get bored, my love." she said breathily, causing him to close his eyes and put his hand to his head in a gesture of supposed agony.

"By God, you torment me, woman…and I love it!" His eyes shone with amusement. "Go slow, I beg you, so that I can savour every second." He took a step back, crossed his arms and, with a small inclination of his head and a wicked smile, signalled for her to begin.

The slow burn within Violet's breast was already making itself felt in her lower regions. She tried to tell herself this was merely business. She tried to act as if it was, but it was hopeless.

All she could feel was fevered anticipation as she worked first the buttons to remove her slim-fitting bodice, then the hooks that kept her swathed skirt in place, until she was clad only in her corset over her combinations.

"Dear God, you're a sight for sore eyes. Let me help you."

Before she had time to respond, Max's hands were on her, stroking the swell of her breasts and contouring her slim waist. He held her to him a moment, tipped her face and gently kissed her lips.

Thinking Max would want to remove her corset and to enjoy the skin to skin contact that was his preference, she turned her back to him and held out the laces.

"Truly, you're a sight for sore eyes. But I'm too impatient for that," he growled, drawing her round to face him. "We'll save that for next time."

Next time. It was music to her ears.

Then Max's hands were on her, stroking the swell of her breasts and contouring her slim waist. He held her to him a moment, tipped her face, and brought his mouth down to hers.

It was like a match to tinder. She'd thought she'd inured herself to the shock of his touch, but this was something altogether different. Like releasing the beast within her; the wounded soul. The wanton lover.

The simple woman thirsting for love.

Stumbling back, Violet fell back upon the bed, Max upon her, their lips still fused while his hands roamed the length of her, seeming to be everywhere at once. Stroking her thighs, smoothing her hair from her face, fondling her nipples.

Finding the sweet, sensitive place at the juncture of her

thighs which made plain how ready and willing she was to receive him.

He kissed her there, each stroke of his tongue sending shudders of longing, pleasure, and anticipation through the core of her; filling her mind with the fevered madness of desire.

She'd never felt more vulnerable. Or full of need.

"Is that where you like it, my sweeting?" he murmured, raising his head a moment and piercing her heart with the intensity of his narrow-eyed gaze.

"Oh yes." Nearly at the pinnacle, it came out as a rasping breath of rapture, before she drew him upwards and insinuated her hand within the linen of his trousers to grasp his rigid shaft. He stiffened and shuddered; closing his eyes and clenching his jaw as she deftly removed the last of his clothing and took him in her mouth.

"Egad, you know how to please a man." He arched his back and touched her hair, gasping his enjoyment until he gently disengaged her, and drew her up so they were eye to eye. "Enough. I want to do this together."

Together. She'd never heard a word so sweet.

He rose above her, caging her body with his, supporting his weight with one hand while he positioned himself at her entrance. Violet lay on her back, her breathing shallow due to the corset she still wore, her body swimming in lustful pleasure.

"And I want you inside me." *So that I can call you all mine, if only for a few moments.*

Smiling wolfishly down at her, he inhaled audibly, stroked her cheek, then penetrated her in one smooth thrust.

"Glorious!" he muttered, frowning as if he were in pain as he began to pound.

Glorious. She whispered the word inside.

It was glorious to feel his energy.

Glorious to be joined as one. Those had been the words of the priest who might really have married them under different circumstances.

She cast away the gloomy reflection, and her heart blossomed. This was for her as much as for him.

Deep. Intense. Strong and masterful. Each thrust unleashing peaks of exquisite pleasure that rose in upward escalations.

Beloved Max. She ran her fingers through his soft, light-brown hair, arching her body, tensing to receive him with each thrust, her body revelling in the act.

He was a king amongst lovers, and he was hers for just tonight.

She would wring from him everything she could—for this was all she could have.

She ran her hands up his flanks and over his hard buttocks while the roiling sensation in her body moved higher. It took possession of her mind, so she was sensible only to the man joined with her. Within her.

Tonight, he was hers alone. He'd pledged himself to her and in return, she was his forever. Not under the law but in her own mind.

Her mind hazed over. She could see only blazing red and stars while every inch of her body buzzed with sensation.

"Oh Max!" With a cry of release, she shattered around him, waves of ecstasy keeping her afloat, otherwise she'd have drowned in wantonness.

Her climax was, it seemed, all that Max needed. With a moan that sounded more anguished than ecstatic, the escalation of his thrusts increased until, with a final cry, he collapsed on top of her, slick with sweat and breathing heavily.

For a long moment he lay there, spent. Heavy, and she

loved it. Until, finally, he rolled off her and lay beside her, still breathing heavily.

"Zounds, Violet, that was the best tupping I've *ever* enjoyed," he gasped, drawing her laughingly within the crook of his arm.

Violet smiled. What else could she do? She was happy in a sense. He cared for her. She knew he did, and that his feelings went deeper and were more sincere than she'd experienced from any man.

She was happy that she'd given him pleasure, and that he'd given her the opportunity to give pleasure to his aunt in a less sullied sense. Miss Thistlethwaite had shown the kind of simple affection that was only a far-distant memory for Violet.

But it had been an important reminder of the goodness of ordinary people when Violet only existed in a world where hearts, minds, and bodies were traded for coin.

"Violet, you're crying."

He sounded genuinely distressed as he raised himself on one elbow and touched his forefinger to the dampness that streamed down her cheeks.

"Please, I want us to be happy together this last night." He tucked his hands beneath her knees and sat up, cradling her like a baby. "Is it the restrictions? The corset? Did I hurt you?" Feverishly he began to unlace her until the heavily boned garment fell away.

And while Violet could breathe more easily, it did nothing to bring her comfort.

"You know perfectly well while I'm crying. You're leaving me. You're going away, and I'll never see you again." She gasped in a breath and put her hands to her eyes. "I can't pretend not to feel what I *do* feel so deeply for you, Max."

He pressed her face against his chest and stroked her hair.

"Violet, I don't know what to say. I've been honest with you from the start."

She scrunched up her eyes, forcing a smile as she opened them, pushing back to look at him. "These are not recriminations, Max. Yes, you've been honest from the start, as I have." She tried to breathe evenly but her emotions would not allow it. "Oh, you've not misled me at all." She raised a hand to stay his words. "I know you have to leave me. I just…" She heaved in another shaky breath. "I just didn't think I'd grow so fond of you."

"Fond of me, are you, eh? Well, I'd hope so in view of all this." He tried to make it into a joke, but he sounded strained. And was quick to realise even he couldn't make light of the affair.

He swallowed. Gravely, he said, "I've just gained my freedom, Violet. After Mabel left me at the altar, I visited you to celebrate the fact that at last my life was my own."

"Yes, Max. You told me that. Before you even undid my top button, you told me exactly why you were paying me to do what you'd never felt able to do before—sow your wild oats. I understand you." Wearily, she ran a hand across her forehead. "I know you could never ally yourself to a woman like me because of what I am."

"No, you're wrong, Violet. I'd be proud to do so…if the circumstances were right. If I wasn't going away…"

She shrugged. "Well, I daresay I couldn't have borne being the secret part of your life and only able to enjoy you when you drew back into the shadows."

"Lord, I'd not take a wife and a mistress, Violet. Surely you understand that about me!"

She laughed. "Oh, so you'd have to decide whether to make me wife *or* mistress then. I think I know your grandfather's views on that."

"He'll have no say over the decisions I make for my

future. No Violet, you know how I feel about you, surely you do." He tapped his heart, his expression earnest. "I've never felt so strongly here about anyone."

"But you're going away."

He couldn't look at her. "You know it's what I've intended since the beginning," he said softly. "My boat sails in two days, and I will be aboard it, heading towards freedom and adventure."

She wilted in his arms. "While I shall be Lord Bainbridge's mistress before the week is over because he offers me the most security I could hope for—and that's thanks to you, Max, for piquing his jealousy. So, something good has come out of all this."

"Violet?" He clearly was disconcerted by her flippancy as she gently disengaged herself from his embrace and swung her legs over the edge of the bed.

She turned, smiling. "Thank you for the most marvellous three weeks of my life, Max. You've given me more than I ever expected."

CHAPTER 14

"My Lord, is there anything final you wish to pack in your trunk before I seal it?"

It took his valet three attempts to gain Max's attention, and then Max could manage only a cursory shake of his head as he reclined upon the sofa doing absolutely nothing for, in truth, he could not quite whip up the enthusiasm he'd expected he'd be feeling for his impending journey. "If I think of anything during my short trip up-country, I'll send a message."

"You're leaving town, my Lord? Am I to accompany you?"

It was hardly surprising Baines sounded so surprised. Max had only just hit upon the idea himself.

His studied the signet ring on his right hand. His father's. His father had been a young blade in his time, so the rumours went. What would he be advising Max?

And would it be advice Max would consider for even a moment? The more Max heard about his reprobate father, the less he wanted to be associated with a young lord renowned for his drink and womanising.

His grandfather, by contrast, was the scrooge of the

family. He certainly was not the man upon whom to model himself.

He noticed Baines was still waiting, and that he seemed rather tense. Max waved a languid hand towards the window; its curtains pulled back to reveal the gloomy day outside.

"I've just had news that our sailing is to be delayed by twenty-four hours. Apparently, there's a storm nearly upon us."

"Yet you propose to go up-country?"

Max sighed. "Either that or drive myself mad waiting here. You know very well all my energies these past three weeks have been directed towards boarding that ship."

He sent Baines a sharp glance at his silence, then chuckled. "I admit there have been diversions." With a sigh, he rose and walked rather aimlessly towards the rain-streaked window. "But that is in the past, and now my future beckons. My wonderful future without my grandfather or anyone else telling me how to live my life," he added, more to himself. He wished he could feel more excited about it.

Forcing a more robust note, he added, "Without the eternal yoke of constraint, I shall throw myself into a surfeit of adventure. And Grandfather will be able to do nothing about it."

"About what, Max?"

Surprised, and considerably disconcerted, Max turned to find Mabel in the doorway advancing towards him, a look of equal surprise upon her face. She looked a little less orderly than usual with her skirts rain-spattered, and the blooms that adorned her bonnet clinging limply to its brim.

"Why, Max; aren't you supposed to be on your wedding tour? But of course." she added, a look of understanding crossing her face as she glanced through the window at the grey sky. "Your sailing has been delayed. Where's Violet?"

Max sent an anxious look in Baines's direction and indicated with a nod that he was dismissed. He took a few steps towards the cluster of seats arranged in front of the fire and indicated for Mabel to sit.

"Not here at the moment," he said, taking a wingback chair opposite her while his mind spun. Mabel would learn the truth one way or another, but as she was none the wiser now, the longer he could keep her in the dark the better. Mabel could be surprisingly indiscreet at times and would be seeing his aunt shortly.

"Visiting her grandmother," he added, with only a split second required for inspiration.

"Goodness, yes; the tyrannical Miss Lilywhite of Ruislip, though that's a bit of a distance, is it not? And why did you not accompany her?"

With raised eyebrows, she went on, "Your aunt was telling me all about the woman, and she sounds grim. Does she not approve of you?" Mabel untied her bonnet and began smoothing her hair as only a very close friend would do in company. "That wind made quite a tangle of it when it blew my bonnet right off my head. Would you please see what you can do to set things straight at the back?"

Obediently, Max rose and went to stand behind the sofa where Mabel sat so he could render the assistance she requested. It was not a surprising thing to be asked in view of their familiarity over so many years, yet he'd never run his hands through her hair.

"What do you want me to do?"

"Goodness, Max; it should be perfectly obvious. Just tidy what needs tidying. Violet is no doubt going to ask you to do this a thousand times, so I suppose you can take directions from me so you won't be *such* a disappointment." She twisted her head to look impishly up at him. "Sweet and pliant that I am, let this be a reminder of how lucky you are that between us, we've finally got your future on the right path." She sighed and stared ahead while Max tucked some errant strands into her coiffure, and she chattered on. "Now we just have to find a husband for me."

Max grunted. He wasn't attending to her last phrase, but rather the words that should have been prophetic regarding his future with Violet.

"I am so glad you found her, Max, even if it was in a shop."

In the midst of repositioning a hairpin, Max blinked as her words entered his consciousness. He'd been too busy imagining it was Violet's lustrous dark locks he was smoothing and fashioning.

"A shop." How he wished it had been a shop. Longing speared him. If Violet were sitting in front of him right now, he'd be burying his face in her hair, unable to resist the temptation of allowing them to roam more adventurously. Maybe they'd find themselves in bed, though at this hour with the servants about it was more likely he'd take her on a jaunt somewhere she'd enjoy. He'd have liked to have shown her *his* London.

"You're lucky times have changed, even in a few short years, Max. Of course, your grandfather lives in the past. He'll still be furious when he learns the truth, but the fact is that it is less uncommon for a shop girl to marry someone like you—especially if she's very beautiful, like Violet, of course. Peers are even marrying actresses these days. Well, Violet's grandmother is perfectly respectable, so it's not like she won't be received."

Max stilled, the truth warring within him. He'd not expected Mabel to be so open-minded. He exhaled. No, she still could not be trusted with the facts. And besides, Violet's grandmother might be a figment of Violet's imagination. He wasn't sure how much pure truth she'd told him. He certainly believed the terrible story of her parents' murder, but what grandmother of any social credibility would do what Miss Lilywhite's had apparently done? While he wanted to believe Violet with all his heart, in every respect, he had to cling to this one doubt as exoneration for him leaving her.

And leave her, he must. He was desperate to flee England with its stifling constraints and forge a different life from the one his grandfather had carved out for him.

Of course, if he had been looking for a wife, he would have contemplated Violet. Despite everything.

But he wasn't, and he needed to pile up the excuses as to why his original course was still the best and only course for him to follow.

"So, when are you expecting Violet? This evening I'd imagine if you are to board tomorrow. I must say, it is taking a risk, but then Violet strikes me as a girl who's not averse to a bit of adventure and risk-taking. Not like me at all." Mabel sounded quite sanguine. Max decided it was safer to remain standing behind her so she couldn't see his face.

Mabel sighed happily. "Oh Max, she is just perfect for you. She is so striking in looks, and bold and brave, which is just what you need. And she's kind, too. Your aunt simply adores her. I do hope I'll see her before the two of you set sail."

Max reached round to hand Mabel her bonnet. "Sadly, you won't, as I'm heading up to Ruislip this evening to bring Violet back," he said. "She's not expecting me to come, but that'll make her smile, eh?"

Mabel agreed, but the smile that came to Max's mind was Violet's.

And that was the reason he had to leave London. Otherwise, the memory of Violet's smile would drive him mad and he'd go and visit her.

And, at this very moment, almost, she was setting herself

up as Lord Bainbridge's mistress. Probably packing up her worldly possessions just as he was.

Mabel glanced at the dark clouds through the window.

"Surely Violet is halfway home already? Ruislip is a goodly distance."

"I'll ride," Max said. "If I leave now, I'll get there before dark and we can take the carriage back together in time to embark."

There was a certain catharsis in action. Not that Max knew, exactly, where he'd go. Certainly not to Ruislip.

"Sorry Mabel, but I must leave now. Do make yourself at home for as long as you like. And give Aunt Euphemia my regards when she's back from Cornwall. I promise I shall write to you both."

HALF AN HOUR LATER AND HE WAS NEARLY ON HIS WAY. MABEL was horrified to see that he was dressed in riding attire when she insisted on farewelling him on the top step.

His horse had been brought round; the eager white mare flicking its ears in the drizzle as she stamped her hooves and snorted in the frosty air. He'd miss the old girl, but there would be compensations in that magical land across the sea.

For a moment, he closed his eyes and tried to imagine the grassy African veldt that had beckoned so powerfully only weeks ago. When that didn't materialise, he conjured up the sparking gold and diamonds that might be the result of a lucky strike in the diggings—once he got there.

But the only gold or diamonds he could envisage were those he'd love to see adorning Violet's creamy white throat.

"You'll catch your death, Max." Mabel hugged herself and stamped her feet to ward off the cold as she stood on the top step. "Violet will understand if you don't come to fetch her.

Let her return in the carriage." She sighed and added a little wistfully, "Though I daresay you can't bear to be away from each other a moment longer."

Max nodded. "Goodbye, Mabel." He held out his hand to his old friend and was pleased when she moved to embrace him. He wanted to know there was no bad blood between them since he didn't know how long it would be before he saw her again.

But her words stayed in his mind. He couldn't bear to be away from Violet *at this moment*, it was true, but he couldn't be with her, either. It would be fatal to see her again, which was why he'd had to resort to some vigorous exercise in this ridiculously inclement weather. Anything to keep himself occupied while he whiled away the time until he could board his ship.

Without any notion of where he was going, he set off in the direction of his grandfather's estate, though of course he had no intention of going there.

But he had to go somewhere and so he headed west. A brisk, hour-long canter in that direction might work off his agitation and he could return later that night to a hot bath, a fortifying whiskey, and then bed where he'd spend his final night under English skies.

He'd have all of tomorrow to make any final preparations, as long as he was at the docks by four in the afternoon.

It was a relief to leave the traffic behind him and to at last be amidst meadowed fields and quiet woods.

He imagined Violet readying herself for Lord Bainbridge, a thought which made him feel physically ill. He hoped the additional funds he'd deposited into her account would make her think more kindly towards him.

Not that he feared on that score. Violet had been remarkably accepting. Some females in her position would have gone all out to stick their claws in as deeply as they could.

They'd have used reproaches and pretended Max had gone back on his word.

Violet, of course, had made it clear how much she wanted him to stay, but she'd done it so sweetly. If Max had had any intention of remaining in England, he *would* have stayed with her.

She was the most beautiful...and the most beautifully *natured*...female he'd ever come across.

The steady drizzle by late afternoon, and the effort it took to avoid the muddy puddles, whose depth he could not gauge, should have taken all his attention yet still his mind wandered back to Viclet.

How he wished he could think of something else. It was too dismal to dwell on her sad life and how much she'd lost.

He passed a hovel on the outskirts of a village and a couple of scrawny, ragged children, each with a dead rabbit slung over his shoulder. Violet was lucky compared with them, he reminded himself. There were thousands of young women in her position and Max, tenderhearted though he was, couldn't play philanthropist to them all.

He'd reasoned this out many times.

Yet, he did wish he could finish up with one last, fitting gesture before he left English soil. A gesture that would bring a little joy and solace to Violet. Something that came from the heart, but which suggested no weakening on his part.

The thought presented itself to him quite suddenly when he saw the name carved into a stone with an arrow pointing in the direction he was travelling, though he was about to turn back.

Ruislip.

It wasn't so great a distance further. In all likelihood, it's where he'd intended to go from the outset, if he was prepared to admit it.

~

BY THE TIME HE REACHED THE TURNOFF FOR RUISLIP, MAX wasn't at all sure it was a good idea to follow his inclination to deviate via the village. What could be gained by it other than a cursory glance at the house where Violet claimed to have spent her last few years? The house of an unloving grandmother who was fast losing her mind, according to his aunt's reports. Max certainly had nothing to say to *her*.

Nevertheless, he left the main road and directed his horse towards the cluster of habitations. Other than what were obviously labourers' dwellings, there were several fine houses on either side of the graveyard.

This was the graveyard in which Violet's sister had been laid to rest. The sky had darkened considerably, but he was already so wet through the weather hardly mattered.

What did matter was executing a lovely, final gesture—laying flowers on Emily Lilywhite's grave. He could write to Violet and describe the charm of her sister's resting place. It would surely give her some comfort. He felt a jolt of warmth at the idea of making Violet happy, and raised his head to survey the area: a few ramshackle, ill-tended graves to his right, and a few rows of neatly tended graves stretching out towards the grey stone church that huddled bleakly amidst grey skies and dull green fields.

He began to walk the rows, searching for the Lilywhite graves, until he found Zebediah Lilywhite—perhaps Violet's grandfather—beneath a hawthorn tree. Beside him were the graves of his son and daughter-in-law. "Died in Cawnpore. In Memory of..." Yes, these were Violet's parents. With their deaths having occurred in India, he'd been unsure if he'd find anything here to mark their passing.

He was also relieved to find evidence Violet had been

telling the truth. But then, that was one of the things he admired about Violet. She was honest.

Honest about her feelings. Honest about her failings.

Yet proud.

He shook his head to clear it when he realised what he was doing—dwelling on Violet much too much when he was about to leave her. He was here to carry out a small gesture to assuage his conscience and make Violet feel better. That was all.

He glanced down at the sorry bunch of flowers he'd picked during his journey to place on Emily's grave.

If he could only find it.

Pulling up his collar against the wind and the rain, he contemplated Elizabeth and James Lilywhite's graves. An adventurous pair, obviously. He was curious to know what had lured them to India. Was it the spoils of trade? The adventure? Had Elizabeth been as willing to leave England as her husband? How had she endured in frontier-like conditions?

Stamping his feet to keep his blood flow going, he checked himself for thinking such things when it was too late. Violet hadn't spoken much about her parents, but there had been little time for idle chitchat during the past three weeks. The raging physical attraction between them had taken centre stage. With more time for contemplation, Max would have liked to have quizzed Violet about her life in India in view of what he might expect in exploring new frontiers in Africa.

A crack of lightning illuminated the old stone church with its rows of crooked headstones. The evening was advancing, and he should be returning to London for his final night there.

Max sent another dubious look at his floral offering as he

leaned over to place them on the moss covering beneath Elizabeth Lilywhite's headstone.

He hesitated. Despite the weather and the late hour, he really should make the effort to find Emily's grave since he'd come so far. Hers was the grave he wanted to tell Violet he'd seen and tended. He needed to describe it to her and assure her it was well tended.

Slowly he retraced his footsteps, scanning the names of every stone in the cemetery, but still he could not find it.

The storm was intensifying; cracks of lightning spearing the sky with greater frequency now. It was madness for him to be delaying his return, and in weather like this it was foolish in the extreme.

Frustrated, he returned to the graves of Violet's parents; put the flowers on Elizabeth's grave, and headed towards his horse which was tethered by the lych-gate.

As he passed beneath the arch, movement caught his eye and he flinched, immediately berating himself for being twitchy in what seemed so much more ghostly only because of the weather.

Glancing down, he realised it was a prone form, lying along the narrow bench, that had moved. He was about to pass on, assuming the huddled bundle was a vagrant or traveller seeking what little sanctuary the narrow, covered area offered from the wild weather.

But it was not an adult, he quickly saw, and as he passed near, the child sat up, gasping, her expression full of terror when she saw him, before she regained her composure, tucking her knees up under her chin, and staring over his shoulder as if he were of no account.

"Should you not be at home?" he asked. He'd thought the child perhaps a gypsy or beggar child, but then saw her clothes were too fine and she was clearly well nourished. A gentleman's daughter? It was an incongruous finding and decidedly concerning to the parents who must surely have no idea she was here.

The girl shrugged. "Maybe," she said, dropping her eyes and tracing a pattern distractedly upon her knee.

"Is it far to go? I can take you," he offered, despite himself. "Your parents will be worried."

She smiled and shook her head. "I don't think so."

She was so dismissive of his help Max was at a loss. How could he leave a child outside in the dark, alone, in a storm? A little girl? Well, no more than ten or eleven. His conscience wouldn't allow it. Her parents would be wild with anxiety. He certainly would be if she were his.

Unwilling to walk on, he cast about for something that might elicit some information from the runaway. She had to have run away, he decided.

"Are you sure you don't want me to take you back to your house?" He indicated the two buildings on either side.

She shrugged but said nothing, evading his look. In the light of the moon, her pale skin had a ghostly pallor, her eyes seeming too large for her face. Framed by strands of wet, dark hair, her forlorn appearance tugged at his heartstrings. He wondered what must have happened to have sent her into such extreme weather.

"You look as if you can't live too far away. Perhaps you can help me. I'm looking for the grave of Emily Lilywhite."

The girl's head jerked up. "*I'm* Emily Lilywhite," she said.

HER EYES WERE SUDDENLY BRIGHT, HER BODY TENSE AS SHE leapt up, craning her neck to look at him. "I think you must mean you're looking for Violet Lilywhite's grave; then I'm afraid you've come to the wrong place, sir. Violet is buried in London."

Max stared for a long moment. "Who told you that?" he asked, already knowing the answer as a terrible weight of premonition weighed upon his shoulders.

"Grandmama." The little girl slumped back onto the bench seat. "Violet is my sister, you see, but she died last year."

Max cleared his throat. "Did your grandmother say... anything else?"

Emily's lip quivered. "Only that Violet had been wicked, and she died a horrible death because of the evil creature she was."

"Have you been to London to see where she's buried?"

The girl ran her hand across her wet cheeks and shook her head. "Grandmama only told me after the funeral, and when I wanted to go and see my sister's resting place she said I'd be contaminated." Dully, she returned to tracing patterns with her finger on her knee.

Seething inside, Max managed to ask, calmly, "What else did she tell you?"

"That not a single person went to Violet's funeral because my sister was a witch with a soul as black as night and everybody was afraid her sin might rub off onto them." Her voice broke. "I don't think Violet was a witch. We didn't see many people, living at Grandmama's, but everyone thought Violet was beautiful. And kind."

"I'd describe your sister like that, too."

"You would?" Emily's head jerked up and she cupped her face. She looked suddenly beautiful and very much like Violet when she was animated like this. "You knew her?"

Max nodded, cautiously, unsure of how much to reveal. The weather was worsening by the minute, and he could hardly keep the child talking while they were both catching their deaths from cold. Torn, he glanced at the road beyond which led to London. He should be returning soon, but he was duty-bound to deliver this child safely to her grand-mother first.

Yet, he was duty-bound to tell her the truth.

And then what?

Field her cries and whimpers when she begged to see Violet, her beloved sister, and he refused?

If he had had the time, he surely would have taken her.

But he didn't have time. And what could he do for Emily, besides whip up her agitation when he was in no position to do anything to actually *help*?

She was looking at him expectantly. As if she were too afraid to speak and break a spell.

Steeling himself, he said, "But first I must take you home."

"To Grandmama?"

To his surprise, Emily laughed, albeit with a short bark of bitterness that seemed at odds with her sweet pretty face. A face that resembled Violet's—*painfully*—with her large blue eyes and heart-shaped chin.

He nodded, but she leaned back against the bench, gripping the lintel of the gate as if he might try to forcibly make her do her bidding.

"Grandmama will not take kindly to receiving me or visitors," she said, "until the angry mood has passed. I'll go back when it's safe."

"But the storm—"

He was now having to shout to be heard above it.

Still, the child shook her head. "I'm safer here than with Grandmama," Emily shouted back. She pulled up the sleeve of her dress and to Max's horror, he saw a deep gash at least three inches long weeping fresh blood along her forearm.

"What happened?" he gasped, feeling suddenly very unsteady on his feet.

"Grandmama flew at me with a knife. It went in a bit, but I got away in time." Her white teeth flashed and she actually smiled. "Luckily, I managed to get the knife away from her before I ran." She reached down by her side, and in a flash of light, Max saw illuminated the long, sharp blade she brandished for him to see.

He was galvanised by horror, shock, and the feeling that if he didn't act right this very moment on what, in fact, his conscience had been dictating for some time, he could never live with himself.

And in the very immediate thought to follow, he realised how very happy such a revelation made him feel.

"You're a very brave girl, Emily," he said, giving her a considering look that made her beam with pleasure. "Do you think you'd be brave enough to hunt lions in Africa?

CHAPTER 15

So, this was her new home. It was elegant indeed, and Violet should have been overjoyed to have swapped the insalubrious surroundings of her Soho residence for the leafy charm of St John's Wood.

A month ago, she would have been, but as she gazed from the fresh chintz curtains blowing the crisp air through the partly open windows, her heart was like a stone lodged in her chest.

Yet, she could not behave with anything that suggested other than the greatest joy and gratitude when Lord Bainbridge visited her later in the day.

He might not be charismatic, handsome, or even terribly charming, but it was purely through his generosity that Violet's future had taken a marginal turn for the better.

Not that she wouldn't be paying for it in her own way, of course. Still, pretending was second nature, so she'd better do an adequate job she supposed of making his lordship feel he was getting the return on his investment that he expected.

Deserved, she reminded herself. Not every gentleman of her acquaintance had been so generous.

Max was different, of course. She tensed, trying to banish all thoughts of him, her attention diverted by the billowing of the curtains caused by a sudden gust of wind. Violet hurried to rescue a china horse from crashing from its place on the windowsill just as there was a knock on the door.

She straightened her skirts, her heart pounding in her chest, and did a quick check in the looking glass above the mantelpiece. Lord Bainbridge was very particular about appearance and everything being orderly. Including Violet.

The face that stared back at her had a rather haunted look. She'd tried to hide the dark smudges under her eyes from her restless last few nights, but in this light, they looked an even greater contrast with her pale, translucent skin.

Resigned, she turned away. Nothing would improve her looks in the seconds it would take to cross the floor, just as nothing would ease the ache in her heart.

Not all the jewels and fine clothes Lord Bainbridge had promised to buy her to augment the beautiful necklace he'd given her two nights before. To celebrate the fact she'd agreed to be his, he'd said as he'd fastened the gold and ruby 'token of his regard' around her neck. As she dropped her hand from pushing back a ringlet that fell across her shoulder, a flash of the simple gold band she still wore to mark her sham wedding was not the thing to make her feel better.

The knock came again—louder and more insistent—even though she'd hardly kept him waiting. She stiffened but checked herself. She couldn't be angry. She'd have to ensure patience and good humour infused her objection to his impertinence, she counselled herself as she flung open the door, saying, "Goodness, but you are—"

Shock robbed her of the words to complete the sentence. For a moment, she could only stare. She'd come face to face with an apparition. Her mind was playing tricks on her. Taunting her.

"Dear Lord, this can't be true," she whispered, her legs suddenly feeling as if they had no substance.

"Violet!"

It was Emily. Not her ghost, for the arms that wrapped about her neck and pulled her down for a fierce hug was definitely flesh and bone.

"You're not dead!"

They spoke at the same time, disbelief shocking Violet into silence while Emily simply said the same words over and over until, with a hiccupping sob, she stepped back to regard her sister with awe. "But you're here!"

"And would have been to see you if Grandmother had not told me that you had died." Violet saw no need to soften the truth as she stepped back into the warmth of the house, drawing her sister with her as she glanced over Emily's shoulder with a frown. For where was her grandmother who must surely have brought her following a crisis of conscience. Oh yes; Violet was very ready to deal with her as required.

"Come in, before you catch your death," she told Emily. "Have you run away?" And then, in horror, "How did you find me? Who told you to find me here?"

A myriad of lurid scenarios swept away her joy at seeing her sister. For what if her association with Violet should taint Emily? What if this was a trick on their grandmother's part to destroy Emily, just as she had her elder grand-daughter?

But then joy was in the ascendant, for Emily was weeping now, and she needed all the comfort she could get, for what horrors might she have endured for her to have arrived, alone and friendless, on Violet's doorstep?

"Oh Violet, you look so beautiful!" Emily finally gasped when her crying had subsided and she took a step away. Her gaze raked the pink-and-cream polonaise Violet wore, its neat bustle festooned in swaths and adorned with bows at the back while the front hugged her shapely figure. Madame and Lord Bainbridge had helped approve this confection and…

Oh Lord, what if her protector should arrive? He was due within the hour. She closed her eyes briefly before staring once more at her sister, realising for the first time that the young girl was dressed in all but rags.

"Did Grandmother throw you onto the streets, Emily?" she gasped, fingering the coarse homespun smock with its inexpert darning in the many places it had simply worn right through. She knew how much Emily had loved pretty clothes and that, as the favourite, their grandmother had indulged her. "Did you walk here? Your hair is wet! Oh Emily, I thought you were dead! What terrible things have happened?"

"Please don't cry, Violet." Emily reached up to cup her sister's face. "A very nice gentleman found me in the rain and took me to an inn where he organised some dry clothes."

"Dear God, no! You went with a stranger!" Violet's strangled cry was interrupted by the closing of the door, and as she raised her face her sense of unreality grew. Max was entering the room, shaking the raindrops from his hat and removing his heavy, damp coat, for water pooled at his feet upon the floorboards.

"No, a very nice gentleman, as your sister just told you," repeated Max, smiling as he took a few steps forward. "I found her in your village churchyard where I'd gone to lay some flowers upon her grave in a gesture that I'd hoped would give you some pleasure." He put his hand on Emily's shoulder. "But instead of a grave, I found something much better, eh Emily?"

Oh, so much better. A joyous gift and piece of magic that he'd magically spun out of the goodness of his kind, kind heart…

Before he left her to go to Africa. Violet's surge of joy was tempered by the reality, then chipped away further when he added, "Ruislip was hardly out of my way. A short detour only."

She blinked. Oh, so he'd been curious to see if she'd been telling the truth about her name and origins.

She put her arms about Emily and drew her against her body, as if she might use her sister as a shield against the pain of impending loss that was growing within. She had Emily—and that was the greatest gift of all—but how would she look after her sister?

And would her heart ever recover from the loss of losing this wonderful, bighearted man who was smiling at her as if he had no idea how devastating this was for her—and who certainly wasn't suffering any pangs at departing from her forever.

"I don't know how to thank you, Max," she managed, her voice breaking before she gasped, this time in fear as the door was flung open, and Lord Bainbridge stood framed upon the threshold; the grey clouds behind throwing him into terrible relief. For what a large man he was.

And not known for his compassionate heart.

Violet hugged Emily even closer and tried to hide her fear. She'd brazen this out. She had to. Even if she no longer cared what became of herself, she had Emily to care for now, and she could only do that if she had the protection of a man.

"What's going on here?" He took a few steps into the room and locked from Emily to Violet, then across at Max. A frown marred his handsome features, and his lips were pressed into a tight line. Violet could feel Emily's fear though the girl remained silent.

"Well, I need no introduction, Bainbridge, but Violet, don't you want to introduce your sister?"

Violet flashed Max an angry look. It was all very well for

him to bombard Violet's lover with the truth when he was blithely stepping out of their lives forever. But what if Violet had been busily hatching a more creative explanation that might work better on soothing Lord Bainbridge's sensibilities?

"Your sister?" Lord Bainbridge said angrily. "You told me she was dead."

Violet heard the suspicion in his tone, inferring that Violet had lied to him. No doubt he'd be wondering what else she might have lied about.

He turned to Max. "What are you doing in my house?"

The sick dismay in Violet's gut worsened. What was Max doing? How could he display such blatant disregard for Violet's welfare when they'd parted as friends? Had she offended him in some way?

She lowered her eyes, unable to bear the scene. She had nothing to contribute. Her fate was in both their hands right now, and she could only pray that Max would handle the situation in a manner that would not incite Lord Bainbridge's ire.

"Reuniting a homeless child with a beloved relative when both had thought the other dead." Max sounded very calm. As if it had been nothing. Or simply all in an afternoon's work.

And yet Violet's life had been turned upside down. She had been delivered the greatest joy she could ever imagine by discovering Emily was alive, but her fear in the immediate moment at how she was going to look after her sister was growing by the second.

No doubt Lord Bainbridge was wondering the same. He'd outlaid a great deal of money to acquire Violet's loving services. He was hardly going to sanction Emily living in this house with her. Not that Violet would have considered that appropriate either. Emily's future prospects would only be tainted by an association with Violet—a kept woman.

"I had hoped for a somewhat different reception, I must say." Lord Bainbridge directed this at Violet, his tone laced with acid.

Violet ran the tip of her tongue over dry lips. She was frightened. How might he react when Max was gone? Would he insist Violet dispatch Emily immediately? But where could she send her? She had so many questions she couldn't ask. Had Grandmother died? Or had she thrown Emily out and Emily had nowhere to go?

"And what do you plan to do with this child? Your sister?" He spoke as if Emily didn't have ears. His nostrils flared, and Violet envisaged what the next few years might be like. She'd have to pander to this man she didn't even like. A man with no compassion.

"Lord Belvedere asked if I was brave enough to shoot a lion. And I am." Emily thrust out her flat chest and looked combative. "He's going to Africa. I think Africa sounds like India. Exciting. Not like here—"

She'd burst out with such bravado, but Lord Bainbridge cut into her words, "Children should not be heard. Violet, this is untenable—"

Now it was Max, interrupting him to say in his previous, measured tone, "I think Emily would do very well in Africa. We've had a good conversation about it during the carriage ride here. Not a very comfortable carriage ride, I must admit, for after I found the child soaking wet and bleeding from an injury inflicted, apparently, by what I would consider a completely unsatisfactory guardian, I hired the only conveyance to be had in town, which was not quite up to standard, was it, Emily?"

"No, there was a rat living in it, and it smelled horrible." The energy had returned to Emily's tone.

"But needs must, and so I brought Emily to you and had hoped I might see you alone in order to invite you to Africa too, Violet." He smiled. "Unfortunately, I must now offer the invitation in company." He glanced at Emily. "I say, Emily, would you mind seeing if you could locate a servant to make some hot chocolate. Something soothing for this cold weather would be rather nice, don't you think?"

With Emily gone, Max seemed to relax. As for Violet, she didn't know what to say.

Go to Africa with him? In what capacity? Her heart somersaulted with the excitement of various possibilities. He was offering her a lifeline. Had he found someone who needed a companion? A governess? By making it clear that Emily could go too, he'd obviously been very creative.

She saw the roiling anger in Lord Bainbridge's eyes, and knew she'd take her chances and whatever Max was offering her, even if it meant swapping her silks and jewels for a lifetime of servitude. An escape to a frontier where her past did not hang like a millstone around her neck was the most tantalising offer she could ever have imagined.

"On my way here, I stopped by Madame Chambon's." Max lowered his voice and glanced at the door through which Emily had exited. "Don't worry, Violet. I left Emily in the carriage while I had a private audience with Madame and quickly executed the transaction that would see both your employer and you, Lord Bainbridge, adequately recompensed."

Violet swallowed. His generosity was considerable. The sum he must have handed over would have been significant. Yet, she felt like a slave being paid for.

"This is preposterous!" Lord Bainbridge burst out. He took a menacing step towards Max, his face mottled with indignation. "I secured this house for Violet only this week." He made a sweeping gesture with his arm. It was, indeed, a handsome house; furnished without concern for expense. Lord Bainbridge had wanted a tiny palace to accommodate his latest prized possession.

His nostrils flared. "I paid Madame Chambon a king's ransom. Violet belongs to me."

Violet kept her expression neutral while she waited tensely, though she cringed inwardly at the crudeness of the situation. Max was about to make an offer. As long as it included Emily, she'd jump at it. And he surely knew Violet well enough to anticipate she'd take a lowlier position if it gave her an independence with the ability to look after her sister. Why else would he have brought Emily here? Why else would he have paid Madame Chambon and recompensed Lord Bainbridge for Violet's services? Max was tender-hearted. When he'd stumbled upon Emily, the child's plight must have tugged at his heartstrings. He'd not have been able to abandon an eleven-year-old under the circumstances.

But with his ship sailing so soon, he'd have had to have worked quickly to make the necessary arrangements that would settle them both in order to ease his conscience.

Max inclined his head. "I think that really depends upon Violet's wishes. Certainly, she may choose to stay with you, though I wouldn't begin to speculate *why* she would wish to. That is between the two of you, and I am not privy to her feelings for you. However, regardless of what you are offering Violet, and in case you didn't quite understand what I thought was very clear, I have come here, with Emily, to recompense you for the expense you have already outlaid and to make Violet a counteroffer."

Lord Bainbridge's eyes bulged. Max's reasonable tone was doing nothing to soothe his ruffled sensibilities.

He squared his shoulders. "You are sailing for Cape Town tomorrow, as everyone knows. Shirking your responsibilities to go adventuring. Seeking your fortune in a new frontier."

He shrugged. "Am I to understand you want a doxy to keep you warm at night and wash your shirts by day?" He snorted. "What can you offer Violet? Certainly not the comforts, the clothes, the jewels that I can."

Violet raised one eyebrow. They meant nothing to her compared with her freedom. Nevertheless, she held her words. It was a tense moment between the two men, and she didn't want to force Max to play his hand earlier than he intended. He'd know very well she'd place a higher value on liberty than on material things, yet she had to eat—and right now the only way she could manage that was through the protection of a man.

Lord Bainbridge was her official protector, and Max had not yet made any firm proposition other than saying he'd paid for Violet's release so she could look after her sister. She assumed that's what he meant.

But Emily's declaration that he'd invited her to Africa and Max's vague affirmation that she was welcome to come was confusing. She doubted he'd offer her something truly demeaning, but until she knew exactly what it was, she would wait.

Nevertheless, her fingers and toes tingled with excitement. If Max wanted her to take her chances and accompany him to South Africa, he'd have come upon some ingenious way to enable her to find employment so she'd not be far away.

Her sister's light, hurried footsteps sounded in the passage and the door burst open. A wave of sisterly love washed over her at the sight of her pretty, earnest sister, importantly and carefully bearing a tray with four steaming mugs.

For so long, she'd believed Emily dead. She still couldn't believe her grandmother had told her such lies.

Now Max was facilitating a way for Violet to keep her

sister close. That was all that was important.

Her excitement drained away. Perhaps Max's counteroffer was to send Emily to school. It would be a kind and generous act when he had no obligation, but he'd know Violet would be resistant. Perhaps that's why he'd not yet put his counteroffer into words.

"So, Emily, would you like me to take you both back to your grandmother?" Max turned to elicit the young girl's thoughts with a smile. "Perhaps she'd be overjoyed to discover that Violet isn't dead."

Emily's eyes widened, and her skin blanched. Silently she shook her head, and the mugs on the tray rattled perilously as she set it down on the sideboard. "No! Grandmama said Violet was dead! She said she wished I was too when she threw the knife at me."

"A flesh wound, yet deep enough." Max spoke matter-of-factly to both Violet and Lord Bainbridge. "I had it dressed when we stopped for dry clothes along the way. The last few hours in the carriage have been very illuminating. Emily's grandmother was once quite respected in her local district. But rumours of her madness appear to be growing, according to the pharmacist who sold me bandages and liniment. Violent, too, it would appear. Increasingly so. No, I would not send Emily back there, and I would not send Violet back, either." He made a gesture of confusion with his hands. "It resulted in quite a conundrum for me. Emily was so very believable and quite engaging, once she'd got herself warm and dry and decided I wasn't a proxy for her wicked grandmother. Indeed, she made a very convincing case for rescuing a damsel in distress." His forehead puckered. "Yes, very convincing. Yet how could this be reconciled by a man who, for the past three weeks, has been counting the days until he can exercise his freedom from all the constraints that make England such a stifling place to be right now."

Emily hurried to his side and looked up at him. "But I told you, Max, that I'd help you. I'm very good at polishing. Grandmama makes me polish all the silver cutlery every week, so I can polish your boots and help you put them on. I have to help dress Grandmama so I'm sure I could help dress—"

"That's very sweet of you!" Violet interrupted quickly, hurrying over to take Emily's hand. "You always were the most biddable of sisters."

"Except when I'm angry! Then, I'm Grandmama's despair," Emily told them all and looking quite proud about it. "But that's better than being timid if I'm going to have to shoot lions, isn't it, Max?"

Violet blinked. Max seemed to have made a very positive impression on her little sister in a few short hours.

"It certainly is, Emily. And that's what decided me. In fact, it was when you angrily told the innkeeper that he'd over-charged me for the mutton roast we both so much enjoyed. His wife had quoted me a shilling, you see," he told the others for their elucidation, "but the innkeeper saw easy coin when he looked at the cut of my gib. At least, that's how Emily phrased it, having, I suspect, lifted the phrase from the pirate novel she'd been reading."

Violet nodded. "Emily is a voracious reader," she murmured. "She loves her adventure stories."

"And I think taking her to Africa to live out a real live adventure rather than having to read about them or make them up would be just the thing."

"You'd have to take me to Africa?" Emily worried at her lip. "You want to take me away? I thought we'd go to...the zoo." She looked from Max to Violet, as if torn.

"I don't mean take just *you* to Africa," Max reassured her with a laugh. "I meant take you and *Violet* to Africa. That's if

Violet agrees to go. It's rather a big decision for her to make considering the boat sails tomorrow."

Lord Bainbridge looked at Violet. "No doubt Violet would have been better swayed had your proposition come from the heart," he said. "Your boat was to have sailed yesterday but was delayed by bad weather. Rather serendipitous the way matters have unfolded, and rather curious, I can't help feeling. I wonder what other considerations you have neglected to inform my mistress."

Violet glared at him. She was more offended by his use of the term in front of Emily than by his casual demeaning of her.

Max, however, seemed highly affronted on her behalf. "How dare you insult the woman I love. It's true I was to have left yesterday, though thank God for whipping up a storm and giving me the time I needed to reflect. Thank God for Emily here, who's helped me understand what I really want. Not adventure and the unshackled freedom I'd thought I did."

He put up a hand for silence, as Lord Bainbridge and Violet both opened their mouths to speak.

Lord Bainbridge spoke anyway. "You are really so puffed up with your own arrogance that you believe your charm will win Violet over so you can drag her across the seas with you as your—"

"Lord Bainbridge, please," Violet murmured with a speaking look in the direction of her sister.

Max rolled his eyes and sent a despairing look at his lordship, then Emily, then finally, Violet.

"I say, Violet, I'm sorry about this. My preference would have been to have spoken in private and to have elicited your wishes, but the fact is I'm going to have to declare myself in front of a crowd, and that does not sit comfortably with me. Nevertheless, here's my offer."

Violet put her hand to her mouth. He was about to declare himself. To say the words that would confirm exactly what he thought of her; how much he valued her. Was she to go as his servant or someone else's? Did he want her to be his mistress as he explored exciting new frontiers, or did he plan to engage her in some other capacity?

The pounding in her chest was so intense she thought she'd be ill. Her nerves felt frayed to breaking point with the anticipation.

She didn't care what his offer was—she'd accept.

"You're a fool if you think you can take him at his word." Lord Bainbridge's snarl sounded an ugly note in the silence.

Violet gave a short laugh. "If there's one thing I know about Max it's that I can take him at his word. He's never been anything but honest and transparent."

"I like that." Max beamed at her, then touched his heart. "It gives me great hope, then, for a favourable answer when I ask you to throw aside everything here so you can marry me and come to South Africa." He glanced at Emily. "Together with your sister, of course."

"*Marry* you?" The world rushed at Violet like a storm engulfing her senses. She managed to remain standing, but Max's face came in and out of focus, his smile ever more charming, while Lord Bainbridge's expression grew increasingly malevolent.

"You believe him? A sham marriage? That's all it would be and you're a fool if you think otherwise, Violet. Men like Max don't marry their—"

"Have you forgotten the company you are in," Max said warningly, looking at Emily who stared, wide-eyed, between them. "And no, sir, it would not be a sham marriage. Violet is clever enough to know the difference. If she had any doubt, I'd be willing to do what it took to prove it to her." He took a step forward and his fingers closed over Violet's. He seemed to have eyes only for her. "I feel like I've been given a second chance. I was supposed to have been on board the *Charlotte* yesterday, but when I woke up this morning, all I could think of was you and how terribly sad I was that I'd not see you again. It's what prompted me to go to the village where your grandmother lives, and when I saw Emily, I knew in my heart I couldn't leave you behind." He squeezed Violet's hand and bent over to elicit Emily's opinion.

"Do you think Violet should say yes? She hasn't said anything, you know, and I'm growing a little concerned that she doesn't think my offer is a very enticing one."

Violet swallowed. It was all too marvellous to be real. She didn't trust herself to speak in case the act of opening her mouth to say the words would prove it was all a dream.

"You want me to be your wife?" she repeated, her voice barely a thread of sound.

"Yes; my legal, wedded, honestly acquired, wife. My beautiful bride." Max touched Violet's cheek lightly, then gave a self-conscious laugh. "Lord, I really didn't think I'd have to propose in front of…of Bainbridge here."

"But it *is* his house, and there isn't much time," Violet whispered.

Max burst out laughing. "Exactly right! You do see matters quite as they are, and I think I shall find that exceedingly refreshing in the years to come." He frowned. "That is, if you do choose to marry me."

He'd said it too many times now for her not to believe him. Bainbridge had opened his mouth to utter some-no-doubt-odious remark, but Violet got in first.

"I would love to marry you, Max. Whenever and wherever you think it appropriate." An incredulous laugh escaped her. This couldn't be real. First Emily and now…this.

"I'm so glad you said yes, Violet!" Emily was clapping her hands, her little face coloured by excitement. "For a moment

I wasn't sure, and Max is quite the nicest man. I'd much rather live with him than Grandmama."

Lord Bainbridge grunted. "It appears I'm superfluous." He sounded more bemused than vindictive, which was what Violet had expected. Perhaps he knew when he'd lost the fight. "And I'd prefer that you not continue this conversation in my house." With a curt nod, he stepped aside and indicated the door. "I hadn't thought you so credulous, my dear. Belvedere speaks of marriage, yet I have no idea how that can be achieved when there's no time for the banns to be called, for one thing, and certainly enough family opposition to sink a ship."

"Which is exactly where our marriage *will* be conducted in the most respectable and natural fashion possible," said Max sounding ridiculously pleased. "The ship's captain will marry us, and Violet will look as stylish as any modern bride. My aunt has already seen to that. Now, enough said for the moment." Max took Violet's hand more firmly, then reached for Emily's. "Come, ladies." He nodded at Bainbridge in dismissal. "I'm sorry for your loss, Bainbridge. But it is my gain. I love Violet. I've loved her from the moment I laid eyes on her and I will love her for the rest of time."

He opened the door, hesitating on the threshold to cup her face, his hands trailing down to the gold chain around her neck.

"I believe this belongs to you, Bainbridge," he murmured, unclasping the 'token' and passing it to his erstwhile colleague without even looking at him.

"Just as Violet belongs to you?" Bainbridge responded with a sneer as the chain pooled in his open palm.

Max shook his head. "Oh no, Violet is her own woman," he said, gazing into her eyes. "I'm just fortunate that she's agreed to make me the happiest man alive."

"Gin and tonic, dear? It certainly is hot."

Violet leant back in her camp chair and closed her eyes, smiling as she fanned herself. "Why not, Aunt?" She turned at the soft tread of boots; clapping her hands in pleasure as Max emerged from the bush and strode across the sand towards them. His gun was slung across his shoulder, and his khakis were streaked with dirt and sweat.

"Emily and I have organised dinner for us, haven't we?" he said to the girl at his side. "And dinner for an entire village since she shot a buffalo, so we've made ourselves very popular in the district. What have you and Aunt Euphemia been doing while we've been gone?" He bent to kiss Violet's brow and murmured for her ears only, "I can't tell you how much I've missed you. And how much I desire an early night."

Pleasure sparked through her as she retained her hold on his hand. "Your aunt and I have been doing a little of this and a little of that and not very much at all, though you should know that she has not had a paroxysm of coughing in two days. I think this hot, dry part of the world really is doing her good."

It had been Max's idea to visit his aunt one last time before they set sail. But it had been Violet's spontaneous suggestion while they were all in her drawing room that she accompany them to a climate that would be conducive to her health.

Aunt Euphemia's acceptance had been hesitant at first, which was only natural since she'd had just four hours in which to pack. Then joyful and touching because, as she stated, and as they all knew, what did she have to look forward to in England?

Less easy to navigate was the information that Violet and Max were not, in fact, legally wed. Miss Thistlethwaite, however, was shrewder than Violet had given her credit for so after her initial surprise, she'd indicated that Violet explain the circumstances, as she chose and in her own words, when the time was right. This had led Violet to imagining her next few days would be spent agonising over how she could illuminate Max's aunt on at least the basics of why Max had not married her properly—and in a manner which would not horrify her.

Only, how *could* she explain her sordid past?

Exposure had come earlier than expected when Miss Thistlethwaite had wanted to reassure herself that Violet had her wedding gown properly packed so that she could wear it for the ship's marriage service.

The truth was that the gown was still at the St John's Wood residence Lord Bainbridge had secured for her, and Violet was too ashamed and afraid to venture over that threshold once more.

But Miss Thistlethwaite had been adamant, saying that in truth, the gown belonged to her, and that she didn't care where it was being kept right now; she intended to reclaim it.

Violet could only breathe a sigh of relief that it wasn't at Madame Chambon's.

So, she and Aunt Euphemia—as the old lady had insisted Violet now call her—had taken a hackney to St John's Wood where, to Violet's horror, they had come upon Lord Bainbridge himself, ensuring that the more valuable pieces of jewellery he'd given Violet had not been taken. He'd managed to keep his anger in check for the sake of the old lady, clearly, but he'd said enough in the time it had taken the maid to fetch the wedding gown, to make clear his arrangement with Violet.

So, Violet's shame was on display. And, although nothing had been said implicitly, Aunt Euphemia now knew that Violet had been kept in sin by another man; a fact corroborated comfortably by Max a short time later when he'd reminded his rather quiet and clearly brooding aunt that he didn't know what else might have become of Violet after her violent and quite mad grandmother had thrown her onto the streets.

Now, as Violet and Aunt Euphemia watched Max and Emily disappearing towards their tents, singing the latest ditty Max had taught his young ward, the old lady sighed as she leaned over to clink glasses with Violet.

"My nephew really does adore you and…" She trailed off, her pale blue eyes having taken on a faraway look. "I imagine affection is all the greater for knowing there are no secrets or skeletons in the closet."

"Because Max knows the worst of my sins yet can still love me? Oh dear, please don't cry Aunt Euphemia." Violet rose and put down her glass, so she could comfort the old woman who'd become so important to her. "Yes, shame is a terrible thing, but I've been so lucky in that Max has known the very worst of me from the very start. It makes what we have now even richer in value to me." She knelt at the foot of the chair and began to stroke the old lady's arm. "Please, there's no need to cry on my behalf. You can see how very happy I am. I…I'm just so sorry to have disappointed you." She was dismayed to think how much worse Aunt Euphemia would think of her if she knew *everything*.

"I'm not disappointed in you in the slightest." Aunt Euphemia's voice was muffled through the lace-edged handkerchief. "It's the fact that my darling nephew was noble enough and intelligent enough to embrace you and your *future*, rather than take your past as the sum of your value. I mean, I… Oh, it doesn't matter."

Violet looked at her, perplexed, for Aunt Euphemia was crying even harder. "What are you trying to say, dearest?" Violet asked soothingly, as she stroked the old lady's cheek. "You can tell me."

Aunt Euphemia took a quivering breath and gripped Violet's wrist. "When I was thirty-five, I did have an opportunity to marry. Septimus and I spent a summer at Tunbridge Wells where I met a kind widower. He wasn't exciting, like Richard. I didn't love him, as I had Richard, but he courted me, and I was ready to accept him."

Violet looked at her with compassion. "But Septimus was determined to ruin your happiness as he had when Richard wanted to marry you?"

"To the contrary, Septimus thought Mr Sparrow was as good a catch as a woman of my advancing years could hope for. For a start, he was rich whereas Richard had been like a bolt of lightning—full of ideas and energy but with no funds behind him."

"But…why did the marriage not go ahead?"

Aunt Euphemia began to cry softly again. "I wanted to confess to him my sins so that we could forge a future with no secrets."

"But Richard was surely not a past secret you needed to be ashamed of," Violet protested.

"Having his baby was."

Violet exhaled sharply. Her limbs felt like jelly. She'd never been so shocked. Or felt such pity. She'd known many girls at Madame Chambon's who had been forced to manage such situations. Fortunately, she'd not been one of them, though she hoped with all her might that not taking the usual precautions would see that she and Max were blessed with children when the time was right.

Aunt Euphemia, by contrast, would have known nothing of sexual matters.

Confused, she clarified, "But...I thought Richard wanted to marry you when you were very young?"

"He did." Aunt Euphemia nodded. "But Septimus gave him short shrift and forbade me to see him. He returned ten years later, and our love for each other was undimmed. But Septimus caught us. He beat Richard without mercy and sent him away. This was twenty-five years ago now, and I've counted each passing month faithfully. I never saw him again." She hung her head and put a hand to her belly. "But nine months later I bore his child. Septimus sent me to a couple in Norfolk. They were kind enough, but in his pay. I never even held my daughter. I was made...*told*...to forget the past, but never to forget my sins. Five years later, when Mr Sparrow came courting me, I believed I could find a kind of contentment with him. I dearly wanted to escape Septimus, and Mr Sparrow seemed so very sympathetic and kind. He said he hoped we would have children someday and was so very sad he'd not been blessed in his previous marriage. In fact, his greatest fear was that we might never have children and that's when I blurted out the fact that I was capable of bearing them; that I *had* borne a child. It was a grave miscalculation and one about which I won't go into detail. Suffice to say, I'm glad I didn't marry a man who couldn't accept my past. You, on the other hand, have found a man who loves you despite the men in your life."

Violet smiled. So, Aunt Euphemia knew there'd been more than one.

"I have indeed. And I've found an aunt—someone who is far dearer to me than my own remaining relative—who has accepted my past, too." She kissed the old lady's cheek. "I can't tell you how much that means to me."

"Just what I like to see! Happy families in the African bush." Max's tone was carefree as he emerged from the nearby tent having just put on the phonograph. A few crackling sounds of a waltz were making themselves heard above the twilight calls of the birds and the distant trumpeting of a herd of elephants. Brahms. Violet recognised the painfully beautiful strains of music.

"Dance with me, my love." He drew Violet into his arms, calling for Emily to finish braiding her hair for dinner as she was needed for an impromptu dance party. "You can partner your old aunt, Emily m'dear. She's looking chirpier than I've seen her in a long time." He nuzzled Violet's ear, sighing in pleasure as he held her close. "You did right in insisting she join us. I wasn't sure her health or her sensibilities were up to it."

Violet wrapped her arms about his neck and melted against the man who'd given her so much and accepted so much. In the three months they'd been exploring South Africa, moving north to the hotter, sandier regions, she'd never felt more unencumbered. She'd left the burden of her past in a more rigid society where she'd not have been accepted, she knew.

But out here, beneath this endless sky that was preparing its final show of beauty before darkness fell, she felt the greatest affinity with her new surroundings.

"I don't think you need to worry on either account. Your aunt's sensibilities are no more or less finely tuned than yours or mine, Max. And she's happy now. Like she's not been in a long time."

Max smiled and kissed her gently on the lips before he tilted his head. For a moment, they both gazed about them in silent wonder—at the camel thorn trees silhouetted against the fast gathering dusk; the pinks and purples of the sunset almost swallowed up by darkness, and at their comfortably furnished tents just beyond a blazing campfire.

Max held her tighter. He gazed into her face; his expression serious. "The first night I met you, Violet, I said I was sailing away from England to find freedom. I thought freedom was leaving behind what had become detestable to me. But I was wrong." He cupped her face, not caring that Emily and his aunt were so close. "Freedom was finding you, Violet. And being allowed to enjoy you in a place where there was no judgement. A place like this." He made a sweeping gesture with his hands then touched his lips to hers. "Look at the beauty of that sunset; all golden and violet. Magnificent and beautiful. Like you. I love you, Violet," he said simply. "I love you for everything that has made you who you are. And I love you for making me realise the kind of man I want to be. Principled and proud of doing what's right. Not an orphan with an exacting grandfather whose rule I must escape but a family man who relishes his unexpected responsibilities." He returned Aunt Euphemia's smile as he moved Violet languidly round the termite mound that punctuated their dance floor, while Brahms' Waltz in A-Flat floated on the breeze.

Violet swallowed past the lump in her throat, her eyelashes damp as he went on, "Responsibilities that include an aunt in her twilight years who surely isn't too old to find herself a diamond magnate or an elephant hunter. Because we are never too old to find love and love can surprise us when we least expect it. And my greatly-adored young sister-in-law who has learnt to shoot a target at 100 yards, and who promises to break as many hearts as there are stars up there."

A few yards away Emily and Aunt Euphemia were giggling at their attempts to coordinate their dance steps. They looked so carefree and happy that Violet was almost overwhelmed by love for them.

"You were so keen to set off with just yourself yet suddenly you were responsible for three women, Max. And you've taken it in such good heart, like the decent, noble, *responsible* man you are." Violet raised herself on her toes and kissed him on the cheek. Warmth spread from her toes and up through her heart and shoulders like liquid honey as Max held her and the achingly poignant sounds of the familiar waltz enveloped them.

"If this is responsibility, my sweet Violet," he murmured, stroking her cheek, "then let me be shackled by it for the rest of my life."

THE END

Would you like to know when I have new releases as well as get the romantic start to my Regency-set 'Dynasty'-inspired *Daughters of Sin* series?

Visit my website at www.beverleyoakley.com to receive a Free Copy of Her Gilded Prison!

Wicked Wager
Her Valentine's Secret

FAIR CYPRIANS OF LONDON Series
Saving Grace
Forsaking Hope
Keeping Faith
Wedding Violet
Christmas Charity

OTHER BOOKS BY BEVERLEY OAKLEY

Beverley Oakley is an Australian author who grew up in the African mountain kingdom of Lesotho, emigrated to South Australia when she was young, and married a Norwegian bush pilot she met while managing a safari lodge in Botswana's Okavango Delta.

Her romance writing career began as a way to amuse herself in the 12 countries she's lived as the 'trailing spouse' of a pilot husband, and when she worked as an airborne geophysical survey operator in the back of low-flying Cessna 404s and CASA 212s – often the only female crew member – in remote locations around the world.

Her *Scandalous Miss Brightwell* series was nominated **Best**

Historical Romance by the *Australian Romance Readers Association*. She is also the author of the popular *Daughters of Sin* series, a Regency-era 'Dynasty-style' family saga laced with intrigue.

Under her real name Beverley Eikli, she writes Africa-set romantic suspense, and psychological historical romances. Her Napoleonic tale of espionage and intrigue *The Reluctant Bride* won UK Publisher Choc-Lit's **Search for an Australian Star** competition and her Regency tale of redemption *The Maid of Milan* was shortlisted in the *Top Ten Reads of 2014* at the **UK Festival of Romance**.

Beverley lives north of Melbourne (overlooking a fabulous Gothic lunatic asylum) with the same gorgeous Norwegian husband, two daughters and a rambunctious Rhodesian Ridgeback.

www.beverleyoakley.com
beverley.oakley@gmail.com

You can also:
Sign up to her newsletter and get a free book here.
Like her on Facebook here.
Follow her on BookBub here.
Visit her Website here.
Visit her Amazon Author page here.